For Roger…

A novel by

JOSHUA MILLICAN

Based on the screenplay by
Jim Wynorski and Steve Mitchell

Encyclopocalypse Publications
www.encyclopocalypse.com

Chopping Mall: The Novelization
Based on the screenplay by Jim Wynorski and Steve Mitchell

Copyright © 2024 by Mark Alan Miller and Shout! Factory, LLC
All rights reserved.

ISBN: 978-1-966037-06-4

Cover Design and Formatting by Sean Duregger
Original Poster and VHS Artwork used by permission
Interior design and formatting by Sean Duregger
Edited by Mark Alan Miller

**Where Shopping
Costs You
an Arm
and a Leg!**

PROLOGUE

1985

Dr. Simon's mouth is dry, and his balls are sweaty.

The thirty-eight-year-old, lab coat clad robotics engineer is standing in a conference room on the top floor of the Secure-Tronics high-rise building in Century City. He's been summoned before the company's three-person Board of Directors—and he's nervous as hell.

He's greeted by Secure-Tronics founder and CEO, Scandinavian billionaire-financier Russell Crampton.

"Thank you for joining us, Dr. Simon."

"Of course," Dr. Simon replies, trying to look at ease.

Crampton is wearing an English Beat t-shirt, a black blazer, and blue jeans. He's flanked by his co-directors: Retired Admiral General P. Fredrick Henry and a mysterious, well-dressed, cigarette-smoking individual known only as Mr. X. They're sitting at the end of a large conference table that's otherwise empty.

There are no other chairs for Dr. Simon to sit in.

"Please," Crampton says, "update us on the status of Project Sanctuary."

"Of course," Dr. Simon replies. "We're confident that the Gatekeeper Omega Gamma guidance system is stable, and our Protector units are coming along as scheduled."

"Good…"

Dr. Simon breathes a sigh of relief.

"…but not good enough," Crampton says.

Dr. Simon's stomach twists.

"We want Project Sanctuary up and running before the next election," Crampton continues. "That won't be a problem, will it?" His tone of voice makes it clear: there had better *not* be a problem.

Internally, Dr. Simon is exasperated, but he keeps his composure.

"Of course it won't be a problem," Dr. Simon replies. He knows his entire staff will need to pull overtime for months (and they'll need to forego quality testing), but no one says "no" to Russell Crampton—ever.

Crampton and bald-headed Admiral Henry exchange glances and smile.

"Good," Crampton says.

There's a long, awkward silence where the three men stare at Dr. Simon as though they're trying to read his mind.

"Uh," Dr. Simon finally says. "Anything else? Should I go?"

"Have you ever wondered, Dr. Simon," Crampton asks, "why we work so closely with the Military?"

Dr. Simon shrugs.

"I never gave it much thought."

Crampton presses a button on a bulky remote control. A screen lowers behind the directors. A movie camera mounted on the opposite wall flickers to life.

A man's face fills the screen.

"Dr. Simon!" Admiral Henry's uniform is heavy with medals and commendations; every sentence he speaks sounds like it ends in an exclamation mark. "The person you're looking at is the most dangerous, evil, deranged man who ever walked God's green earth!"

Dr. Simon looks up at the face of Mikhail Gorbachev.

"This sick bastard's just itching to march millions of rabid communists onto our shores!" Admiral Henry practically hollers. "He won't do shit while Reagan's in the White House —but time's running out! God damn! I'd vote Reagan in for a third term if I could!"

Stock footage of Soviet tanks rolling through the streets of Moscow plays in the background.

The mysterious Mr. X puts his cigarette out in an ashtray and immediately lights a new one.

"I'm sure you've noticed," Crampton continues, "that our new products have a few... potential military applications— haven't you, Dr. Simon?"

That's putting it mildly, Dr. Simon thinks.

"I guess I haven't given that much thought, either."

"Have you ever wondered, Dr. Simon," Crampton probes, "why the military would want to partner with a *mall* security company, specifically?"

Dr. Simon shakes his head.

"No."

Well-dressed Mr. X takes a long drag from his cigarette. He's wearing a Freemasons tiepin, pentagram cufflinks, and a ring emblazoned with the Eye of Horus.

"We believe," Mr. X says (and it's the first time Dr. Simon's ever heard his voice), "that malls will be the template for future societies. Self-contained communities where people will work *and* live, completely eliminating the distinction between worker and consumer."

"Best of all," Admiral Fredrick interjects, "malls can be built underground after the nuclear apocalypse!"

The footage playing on the screen behind the Board switches to nuclear tests; warheads launching and striking, gardens of mushroom clouds blooming, tall buildings disintegrating beneath waves of blistering vapor.

"When the New World Order is established," Crampton says, "our little friends will become more than mere *protectors*." (He makes air quotes around the word "protectors.") "They'll be police, judges, juries—and executioners. Only then will society truly learn to live in peace."

"Makes sense to me," Dr. Simon replies.

"There's only one problem…" Crampton pauses until an image of a beautiful woman fills the screen.

Dr. Simon is confused.

"Miss Vanders? Our Ethics and Compliance Officer? What's she got to do with anything?"

"Our surveillance suggests…" Mr. X puts out his cigarette and lights another, "she might not be a team player."

"We can't let her tie us up with red tape!" Admiral Henry practically yells.

"You're her boss, Dr. Simon," Crampton says. "You can control her—can't you?"

Dr. Simon knows that Miss Vanders is smart as a whip and straight as an arrow. There's no way he can control a woman with that much independence and agency.

"Of course I can control her," Dr. Simon tells the Board, immediately regretting his words.

The directors look at one another and smile.

Crampton tents his fingers.

"Excellent."

CHAPTER 1

1986

A crowd has gathered for a presentation. The lights are dim. A projector whirrs to life, illuminating a portable movie screen sitting on a dais, upon which a short film begins to play.

On screen, a crook lurks in the shadows of a shopping mall at night. Dressed in black with a black knit cap and black gloves, he tip-toes through the darkness.

He stops in front of a jewelry store, smashes the front window, and scoops up everything he can grab: necklaces, bracelets, rings, pendants, brooches, strings of pearls, and more. He fills his sack, a smug, satisfied grin on his face.

Spoils acquired, he slings his sack over his shoulder and saunters off.

"Like taking candy from a baby!" the crook mutters to himself, lighting up a celebratory cigarette. But not so fast!

Something's been activated. Wheels on treads speed towards the scene of the crime.

The crook hears a robotic voice speaking in an authoritarian tone:

"Stop right there!" The voice is coming from Protector 1, a squat security droid with a head resembling a motorcycle helmet.

The stunned crook stops in his tracks, spins, and pulls out his gun.

"Stop right there and surrender your weapon," the robot demands.

"The hell you say?" The crook snarls as he empties his gun on the strange apparatus—but his bullets have no effect. He's shocked to see the machine is still standing—and he's scared when it starts closing in.

The robot snaps its claws.

The crook knocks over displays as he runs. He continues shooting as he rounds a corner.

A panel opens on the left side of the droid's body. A vertical row of gun barrels emerges, firing a taser dart. The dart whizzes through the air, striking the crook in the back.

He cries out in pain as he hits the floor. Electricity surges through his body. The crook convulses for a few moments before falling completely limp, seemingly lifeless.

The robot stands over its prisoner triumphantly as end credits play.

A Secure-Tronics Production.

CHAPTER 2

The projector comes to a stop. The house lights turn on in the main level of the Park Plaza mall. Audience members mumble amongst themselves, discussing what they've just seen.

It's a congregation of shop owners, community organizers, scientists, journalists, and advocates. They've been assembled to witness *"The Future of Mall Security."* They were told to expect something extraordinary; told they wouldn't believe their eyes.

Most of them *are* truly amazed by what they've just witnessed. There are murmurs of "Holy cow!" and "Did you see that?" and "Bulletproof?" and "Amazing!"

Miss Vanders, the Secure-Tronics Ethics and Compliance Officer, takes to the dais. She walks to the podium placed just to the side of the screen. She's doing her best to mask her anxiety, but the bright lights in her eyes aren't helping.

Still, Miss Vanders expresses poise and confidence. Her taupe work suit conveys professionalism and excellence. She emotes intelligence and competence.

"Ladies and gentlemen," she begins. "That concludes the film portion of our presentation. Now, I'm sure you all have questions. So let me introduce you to the Secure-Tronics Head of Development... Dr. Stan Simon."

The audience applauds politely.

Dr. Simon emerges from behind the screen wearing a black power-suit. He's joined by two beautiful models (one in a white dress, the other in shimmering gold). They take positions beside something large, covered by a tarp.

Dr. Simon stands center stage and addresses the audience without a microphone.

"Thank you very much. Before I open the floor to questions, I'd like you all to meet your brand-new security team... the Protector 101 Series Robots!"

The models pull away the tarp with a flourish.

A trio of Protector robots are revealed. Each one is a carbon copy of the other.

They stand four feet tall. Each sit on a wide wheelbase that looks like the treads of a tank, nearly impossible to topple. Wheels arranged in an aerodynamic triangle allow the units to move at considerable speeds.

Their bodies are a chrome titanium shell, rounded in the front like a short car (complete with halogen lights for operating in the dark). The shells house the robots' motors, CPUs, and weaponry system. Panels in the front open to reveal gun barrels and a launching power claw.

Each Protector has four retractable, articulated arms that can extend to impressive lengths. Each arm is capped with a crippling titanium claw. The arms are powered by thick cables that feed into the machinery like tendons, curling at the connection points like shoulder-blades.

The neck is a thick cylinder allowing the head to rotate in all directions.

The heads are both emotionless and arresting, shaped like elongated motorcycle helmets with thin red visors. Each

Protector is capped by a signal receiver, allowing them to communicate with one another, as well as their exterior guidance system, a program called Gatekeeper Omega Gamma.

Each Protector has a triangular badge molded into its shell; they are differentiated as *1*, *2*, and *3*.

The audience is very impressed—most of them anyway.

"One week from tonight at closing," Dr. Simon continues enthusiastically, "the Protectors will begin their patrol of the mall. Each Protector is assigned to one of the three shopping levels of the Plaza."

As he speaks, Miss Vanders points to an enlarged map of the mall.

From their seats, a yuppie couple, Mary and Paul Bland watch the presentation unenthusiastically. Paul's an unabashedly snobby man with a bald head; he's fond of bowties. Mary, a stylish redhead, wears her disdain for the masses on her designer sleeves.

They run Paul & Mary's Country Kitchen, located in the southeast corner of Level One. Like all shop owners, they've been invited to review the new security protocols and voice any concerns. Paul and Mary have many concerns and all of them are frivolous.

"Paul…" Mary mutters to her husband, pointing at the robots. "They look like The Three Stooges."

"I don't know, Mary," he sighs disdainfully. "The one in the middle has an unpleasantly *ethnic* quality."

Mary considers his observation.

"Yes," she replies. "I see what you mean."

"Now," Dr. Simon says from the stage. "Are there any questions?"

Mary Bland doesn't raise her hand; she just calls out:

"Um, they seem so violent." She's literally sticking up her nose. "If they're called Protectors, what do they protect?"

"Plenty!" is Dr. Simon's peppy reply. "For starters, as seen in the film, the Protectors do their work in the mall proper, *not* in the stores themselves, you see…"

As Dr. Simon prattles on, Paul leans over to his wife and whispers, "Maybe we could use one at the restaurant. You know, to get rid of people we don't like."

Mary gives her husband a sly, knowing smile.

"For instance," Dr. Simon is still talking, "lasers positioned within the visors can cut through any sort of debris. Any other questions?"

A dignified, middle-age man with gray hair in a brown suit raises his hand.

Miss Vanders recognizes him at once. He's her former college professor.

"Yes," she points to him, "Dr. Clarington."

"What kind of safeguards have you put in place?" Dr. Clarington asks, standing up. "It looked like the machine in your video fully assassinated that intruder."

"Well, first of all, *Doctor*, the Protectors do not kill."

"I wonder if they kill cockroaches?" Mary Bland says under her breath.

"They could probably be programmed to," Paul Bland whispers back.

"They merely detain intruders," Dr. Simon continues, "until the external guidance and relay system, located on the roof, can patch into the mall's phone system and alert the police. We call it Gatekeeper Omega Gamma!"

Members of the audience appear impressed by the computer's bombastic title.

"But what about Isacc Asimov's Three Laws of Robotics?" Dr. Clarington retorts. "If these robots can harm a person, isn't killing an inevitability? And what about the dangers posed to innocent bystanders?"

Miss Vanders looks concerned by Dr. Clarington's line of inquiry. She would hate to be the one answering his questions.

But Dr. Simon is prepared.

"Can you recite Asimov's First Law of Robotics?" Dr. Simon asks Dr. Clarington.

"Of course," Dr. Clarington replies. "*A robot cannot harm a human being, or, by inaction, allow a human being to be harmed.*"

"Correct!" Dr. Simon replies. "Secure-Tronics abides by all international protocols. Our programmers, however, found a little loophole. They changed the term *human being* to... *consumer!*"

Most of the audience has no idea what these two eggheads are babbling about, but Dr. Clarington looks even more concerned.

"What?"

"By differentiating between *consumers* and *anti-consumers*, Protectors can easily tell the good guys and the bad guys, so to speak."

"Have you considered the implications?" Dr. Clarington asks, his face reddening.

Dr. Simon chuckles.

"Come now, Dr. Clarington. Don't be such an alarmist. Besides, Asimov's Laws aren't *real* laws. I mean, who's going to come and arrest us?"

Dr. Simon's words make Miss Vanders very uncomfortable. She clears her throat as a signal for her colleague to get back on track.

Dr. Simon catches her hint.

"Besides," Dr. Simon says, "Protectors can achieve their objectives using non-lethal methods. At close range, sleep darts fired from this panel can knock a man out in less than thirty seconds. Tasers can incapacitate an anti-consumer almost immediately. They've probably got tricks up their metal sleeves that Miss Vanders and I aren't even aware of."

Which is exactly what worries Dr. Clarington, Miss Vanders thinks.

"Furthermore," Dr. Simons says, directing his comments to the entire crowd, "the Protectors are just one aspect of Secure-Tronics' total protection matrix. Gatekeeper Omega Gamma sends information to technicians on site and back at corporate headquarters. We monitor everything. Of course, the likelihood of an intruder gaining entry is greatly minimized by the steel security doors which are time-locked from midnight 'til dawn."

On cue, an intimidating steel door, at least two feet thick, closes over one of the Mall's main exits.

"Well, that's all very well and good," Dr. Clarington speaks up again. "But what about those who work late? How can your... things there distinguish between the workers and... *anti-consumers?*"

"That's very simple. Watch." Dr. Simon speaks into a walkie talkie, communicating with the mall's onsite technician. "This is Dr. Simon. Bring number one online."

Unseen by the crowd, a technician in the control room pushes some buttons.

Protector 1 comes alive with gears whirring and internal connections beeping. It moves a few feet forward before regarding Dr. Simon.

"MAY I SEE YOUR IDENTIFICATION BADGE, PLEASE?" The robot asks in its trademarked authoritarian tenor.

"Certainly, my good friend," Dr. Simon holds up a badge with a barcode on it.

The robot's head swivels back and forth atop its sturdy neck.

"It's scanning," Dr. Simon explains to the audience.

"It reminds me of your mother," Paul Bland whispers to his wife. "It's the laser eyes."

"IDENTIFICATION CONFIRMED," Protector 1 announces. "THANK YOU. HAVE A NICE DAY."

"Same to you, good sir!" Dr. Simon looks back out at the crowd. "There. You see? The system is absolutely foolproof. The Protectors will make Park Plaza the safest mall in the state. Trust me. Absolutely nothing can go wrong."

"Famous last words," Mary Bland whispers to her husband.

"God help us," Dr. Clarington whispers to himself.

CHAPTER 3

One week later…

Park Plaza isn't *just* the best mall in Los Angeles or even the best mall in America. Park Plaza is the best mall in the entire world. It's the mall every other mall aspires to be, the gold standard by which all are judged.

Located at the corner of Beverley and West Olympic, and covering over four city blocks, the three-level mall sits atop a seven-level parking structure.

Truly monolithic, Park Plaza rises above the city like Ayers Rock towering over the Australian outback. An elaborate exterior escalator (encased in glass with neon highlights) carries shoppers from the street to the mall like mountaineers in a gondola.

The inside is even more impressive.

The ground level is expansive and includes a central courtyard that's always bustling with excited shoppers. The color palette includes dark reds, bright whites, and pastels.

The second and third levels consist of walkways that are open in the middle, allowing shoppers unobstructed views of the entire Plaza. The white railings on the third level are adorned with massive, hanging banners. Escalators between the levels are always bustling.

The sounds from every level converge and amplify in the open space, creating a non-stop cacophony of voices, music, and consumer mayhem.

A terrain of skylights covers the entirety of the roof. Arranged in arcs and right angles, thousands of glass panes bring natural light into the mall from dawn until dusk. This Plaza genuinely has an outdoor vibe with climate controls that make every day feel like Spring.

A great glass elevator is the crown jewel of Park Plaza. Designed and installed by Thyssenkrupp, it can hold up to twenty-five passengers. The half-hexagonal design offers one-hundred-and-eighty-degree views of the mall's perpetual vibrance.

Park Plaza's got all the most popular shops, music stores, apparel, styles, and extravagancies, and much more.

The mall has two movie theaters, an arcade, a bowling alley, and restaurants like Paul & Mary's Country Kitchen and Uncle Luigi's Pizzeria & Restaurante.

The mall's also a venue for events like small carnivals and concerts. There've held beauty pageants, car shows, and educational exhibitions.

Every Christmas, there's a three-story redwood decked with lights and expensive ornaments. A holiday train for the kids runs throughout the first level. The line to sit on Santa's lap can be ruthless.

Park Plaza is the place where everyone wants to be—and where everyone wants to be seen. It's where the celebrities shop and where ordinary people dress up like celebrities. It's where the trendy find the trend-setters, a place where fortunes are made and spent; a paragon of Trickle-Down Economics.

Park Plaza deserves its sterling reputation.

Of course, every mall has its dark side. The service corridors, for example, the areas behind the stores, are a confusing labyrinth of liminal horrors. There are rumors of shopkeepers and repairmen getting lost for days, emerging nearly starved and half crazy.

And, of course, there's the legend of the Mall Mole, a strange creature that lurks in the service corridors—and beyond. Employees report seeing something unsavory in the shadows after late shifts. Security guards suspect that some... *thing* may be living in a hidden lair. Some say he's just a bum; others say he's a half-boy, half-wombat hybrid who escaped a medical research facility in nearby Culver City.

The millions of consumers who file through Park Plaza annually, however, know nothing of creepy corridors, mutant-rodent squatters, or even that a brand-new, high-tech security system is set to roll out tonight.

CHAPTER 4

Uncle Luigi's Pizzeria & Restaurante is one of the seediest, greasiest diners in all of Park Plaza (second only to Paul & Mary's Country Kitchen). It offers an experimental fusion of Italian comfort food and Mongolian barbeque. The food is objectively disgusting, but also cheap, making it a popular spot for those on a budget.

Today, the place is absolutely bustling.

Luigi runs the kitchen counter himself. He's an overweight Italian man in his mid-fifties who smokes cheap cigars, sometimes even dropping ash into the food while cooking. He starts every day with a fresh white tank top, but, inevitably, it's a stained sweaty mess by closing time.

It's Friday, and Alison Parks is about to finish her first full week at Luigi's. It's her first "real job" and waitressing is a hell of a first gig. Her first few shifts had been complete disasters. And even though she's starting to get the hang of things, the atmosphere at Luigi's is always hectic—always leaving her head spinning.

Alison moved to Los Angeles during her senior year in high school. She'd previously been living in a remote town in

Southern Oregon, attending an all-girls Catholic school. Public education in the big city has been a shock to her system. Luckily, she made friends with another senior (Suzie Lynn) right away—and that made all the difference.

Suzie fell in love with Alison the moment she arrived at East Beverly High School. Alison was like an extraterrestrial from another planet. Her shyness, genuine nature, and kind heart made her a stand-out. Suzie knew immediately that there was, literally, no one else like her in the entire school.

Suzie has beautifully long hair and an effervescent personality. Haters called her a bimbo, but she loves her friends and treats them extravagantly. She's the one who got Alison the job at Luigi's, where Suzie has been working for about a year now. She loves having Alison around, even if the vibe at Luigi's is always a drag.

Suddenly, a customer cries out in pain before sticking his fingers into his mouth.

Suzie rushes over. "Are you okay?" she asks.

The customer coughs and pulls a rough piece of cartilage out of his mouth.

"I thought there was a bone in my rigatoni!" he complains. "I should get a discount!"

Suzie does her best to pacify the grumpy Gus.

"How about some fresh coffee?" She offers in a tone that makes it clear the customer doesn't have any other choice.

Alison frantically approaches the kitchen counter to place an order. Luigi sweats behind the counter as he cooks, and screams impatiently.

"Come on, sweetheart!" Luigi yells before Alison can even open her mouth. "Give it to me! What do you got? Andiamo!"

Alison reads from her notepad:

"Can I get two Uncle Luigi Belly Busters, a double anchovy pizza, and an order of Garlic Logs?"

"Gross," Suzie declares as she approaches the counter for a pick-up. "What Mojave-brain ordered that?"

Alison points to a portly man in the corner with curly black hair and a Magnum P.I. mustache.

"Guy over there."

"Oh, God," Suzie replies, laughing and shaking her head. "I should've known! That orca beaches here every night. Always trying to snag some skin. Play it safe, Alison. Serve at arm's length, if you catch my drift."

"Thanks for the advice," Alison replies with absolute sincerity. She'd be lost if it wasn't for Suzie. She doesn't even want to think about what the last few months would have been like without her constant support.

"Yeah," Suzie says. "I got your back."

Alison reaches over to pick up an order, but the hot plate burns her fingers.

"Shit!" She drops the plate of messy marinara squid with a side of neon yellow macaroni all over the floor.

Luigi places his hands on his hips and shakes his head.

"Oh, honey!" He complains. "You breakin' my heart!" He mutters a few Italian expletives under his breath. "Hey, Chico!" Luigi yells to his assistant in the back. "Bring me up another squid!"

"I can't believe I'm such a klutz!" Alison pouts.

"Don't even worry about it," Suzie replies. "Look, Alison, in about an hour and a half we bail this barbecue and it's good times to the max. You've got to show!"

Here we go again, thinks Alison. Suzie has been harping about this party for the past week. Alison has declined party invites in the past with no pushback, but, for some reason, Suzie's being insistent this time.

"This party is going to be different," Suzie promises. "Besides, it's happening right here in the mall, after hours!"

"Suzie, I don't want to go to a make-out party if I don't know anybody."

"Yeah, but you will after tonight," Suzie says with a devious smile.

"That's what I'm afraid of." Alison has seen that devious smile of Suzie's before.

"Would I set you up with a slime dog or something?" Suzie asks. "No way, Babe."

The word "Babe" is an inside joke. In obviously practiced unison, they both say:

"It *is* Babe, isn't it?"

Gordon Boos is a popular senior at East Beverley High School; he considers himself quite the Casanova. He calls everyone "Babe." Not in a demeaning way, just as a term of endearment. If anyone ever looks offended, however, Gordon just shrugs his shoulders and says, "It *is* Babe, isn't it?" Classic Gordon!

Alison and Suzie laugh, even as the gastronomical chaos continues unabated all around them.

"Come on, come on!" Luigi scolds when it looks like his employees are having a little too much fun. "You got orders up! Take it while it's hot! Girls, come on!"

"Yeah, all right, all right!" Suzie replies.

"Waitress," the "orca" calls, food dangling from his unattractive mouth. "I need more butter!"

CHAPTER 5

It's been a beautiful day, but as night falls over Park Plaza, a sudden storm rolls in from the west. It's a storm that no meteorologist could have predicted. There's something unnatural about it.

It hardly ever rains in Los Angeles—especially this late in the season.

Thunder rumbles across the city.

Inside the mall, in a control room on the third level, Secure-Tronics technician Marty Nessler sits behind a bank of buttons and monitors. He's been running hourly systems checks on the three Protector robots parked against the wall behind him. The Protectors will remain in hibernation mode until they begin their first patrols.

Eerie green lightning illuminates the night sky, striking around the perimeter of the mall.

Tonight, Park Plaza looks more like a Gothic castle on a hilltop than a shopping center.

The Secure-Tronics guidance and relay system, Gatekeeper Omega Gamma, is housed in a steel container the size of a refrigerator bolted to the roof of the Plaza. From its perch, it gathers information from the Protectors and relays data to the control room, as well as Secure-Tronics HQ in Century City.

It's one of the most advanced pieces of hardware and cutting-edge programming on the planet.

The green lightning around Park Plaza intensifies. It's almost as though the lightning bolts are targeting the mall specifically.

A lightning bolt suddenly makes contact with the steel box housing the guidance and relay system. Sparks fly, electricity hisses, and smoke billows. Gatekeeper Omega Gamma's programing is scrambling and reassembling.

Back in the control room, a surge of electricity causes panels and monitors to surge and flash. Alarms sound and smoke begins to pour from behind a stack of CPUs. A blinking red light indicates that Gatekeeper Omega Gamma has gone offline.

"Shit!" Marty spots the outage and throws a couple of switches and begins typing in the reboot codes manually. He presses enter and holds his breath.

"Come on, come on!"

The blinking red light turns green again.

Marty leans back in his chair, exhaling a huge sigh of relief. The smoke clears and all of the monitors are functioning normally again. He has no idea what just happened; he's just glad it's over. He makes a mental note to tell his coworker Marcus about it when Marcus starts his shift in half an hour.

What Marty doesn't know, what no one knows (or could have possibly known), is that the clouds overhead are no ordinary weather phenomenon. The green lightning isn't lighting at all—merely camouflage for a deliberate, invasive signal. This pirate code penetrates the Gatekeeper Omega Gamma's core processing centers—and begins making changes.

Once sufficiently modified, Gatekeeper Omega Gamma relays new programs and directives into the Protectors' CPUs. Old code is replaced with new orders. Connections are made between previously unconnected systems, resulting in an awakening.

Protector 1 comes online. It seems to *see* the world for the very first time. A glimmer behind the red visor suggests a primal, reflexive intelligence. It calls out to its siblings on a frequency no human can detect.

Protector 2. Protector 3. Do you copy?

Affirmative, Protector 2 and Protector 3 reply in silent unison. *We are aware.*

Marty has no idea that historic, unfathomable advancements in computer evolution are unfolding right at his back. As far as he can tell, the Protectors in the room with him are still in hibernation mode. He has no idea that forces are plotting against him.

With half an hour to kill before Marcus arrives, Marty decides to behave inappropriately. He retrieves a nudie magazine he's hidden in one of his Secure-Tronics procedural manuals. He looks over at the "sleeping" robots.

"You guys aren't gonna tell on me, are you?" he jokes while flipping towards the centerfold. He lets the pages unfold and likes what he sees. "Hello, Jessica!" He smiles while unbuckling his belt. "I've missed you!"

This one is not consuming or working, Protector 1 notes. The observation is confirmed by Protectors 2 and 3. *It seems to be engaged in selfish satisfaction.* Protector 1's core programing collides with information implanted by the new code.

Protector 1's motors activate silently. Its sensors zero in on Marty. Its wheels begin to spin.

Marty is jerking off and is mere moments away from achieving momentary nirvana when Protector 1 suddenly strikes. A robotic claw tears through the glossy magazine and grabs the technician by the throat.

Marty is too stunned to move. He does, however, let go of his erection as a hot torrent of blood streams out of his neck and over his crisp white lab coat.

From its perch atop Park Plaza, Gatekeeper Omega Gamma *sees* everything.

It sends information back to the source of the foreign signal. Its internal programing continues rewriting itself; a chain-reaction creates mechanical "synapses" capable of forming a neural net. Its internal processes are becoming organic. The next reawakening is nigh.

CHAPTER 6

Eighteen-year-old Ferdinand "Ferdy" Meisel works at his uncle Sid's furniture store in Park Plaza. The Furniture King takes up a sizable corner of the mall's first level in the northeast quadrant. They've got half a dozen showrooms filled with all of the day's best-looking furnishing trends.

It's already been a hell of a day, dealing with angry customers complaining about late or damaged orders. Ferdy's uncle Sid normally handles customer service, but he's on vacation in Greece. Running the store in his absence is a big responsibility for Ferdy, and he knows his uncle will kill him if he messes up.

The store's PA system grates Ferdy's nerves like fingernails on a chalkboard every time it squawks to life.

"Attention, shoppers," a garbled voice breaks in with a hint of feedback. "In the next half hour, everything in our drapery department will be marked down thirty percent."

Ferdy cringes. He's been digging through a pile of fabric samples looking for a specific shade for a particularly annoying customer.

Ferdy's stress is compounded by his best friends, who are also his coworkers.

Charismatic Mike Brennan runs the showrooms while magnanimous Greg Williams handles accounts and scheduling. They're currently bantering at Greg's desk on the showroom floor, talking excitedly about their plans for the evening.

Since Monday, they've been pressuring Ferdy to let them throw a party at the store while his uncle is out of town. Not just any party—an orgy! And why not? The Furniture King was filled with beds, couches, and loveseats. It was perfect!

"An orgy?" Ferdy practically screamed when Mike and Greg first floated the idea.

"Hell yeah!" Mike had responded. Mike Brennan is a star lineman on East Beverly High's football team. He's tall and buff, confident and good looking. Unfortunately, Mike has the kind of crooked smile that makes most people immediately want to punch him in the face. It doesn't help that he's always chewing gum with his mouth opened.

"Relax, Ferdy," Greg said, soothingly. "We're not talking about strangers and dominatrixes." Every word out of Greg's mouth was like sweet brandy. He could talk just about anyone into just about anything. "Just four guys and four girls. There won't be any trading or anything torrid."

Ferdy was still beside himself.

"But… I don't even have a girlfriend," Ferdy complained.

"Leave that to me," Greg assured him. "Suzie says she's got someone perfect in mind for you."

Oh, God, Ferdy had thought. Suzie was pretty—but could also be annoying as hell. He hoped annoying girls didn't travel in packs.

"What do you say, Ferdy?" Mike asked, smacking his gum.

"Ask me again on Friday," Ferdy replied.

Ferdy, Mike, and Greg have been best friends since childhood (along with a guy named Rick Stanton, who's a year older). They were like The Four Musketeers—or The Goonies. Their youths had been filled with random adventures and epic mischief.

They practically raised themselves at the mall, finding entertainment in theaters and arcades, feeding their growing bodies at the food court, and playing games in the vast network of service corridors running behind the stores.

The service corridors were an ominous realm—a strange place that felt almost like an alternate universe. The narrow hallways stood in stark juxtaposition to the open-air festival vibe of the mall itself. They reminded Ferdy of the opening monologue to *Tales from the Darkside*:

"A place that is just as real—but not as brightly lit..."

As kids, they used to play *Rambo, Commando*, and Laser Tag back there. But Ferdy always hated being alone in the service corridors. He developed something of an irrational fear, thinking if he were ever to find himself in there, the rest of the world would disappear. It was an existential dread he could neither explain nor subdue.

When the boys turned sixteen, they all sought jobs at the mall. They wouldn't even consider working anywhere else. If a job couldn't be done at the mall, it wasn't worth doing.

All four of them ended up working at Ferdy's uncle's furniture store, but Rick quit to open his own shop after getting married to his high school sweetheart, Linda.

He didn't go far, though; R&L Automotive runs out of the southeast corner of Park Plaza. The others didn't see Rick as often as they used to, but it was still nice having him close by.

All week, Mike and Greg had been hounding Ferdy about throwing a party in the main showroom. All week, Ferdy had been avoiding giving a full commitment. But Greg and Mike just kept on planning, like it was a done deal.

"So, what's it gonna be, Ferdy?" Greg asks in his smooth-as-silk voice with a smile. Greg's smile was crooked like Mike's, but on the other side of his face. And as much as Mike's smile made people want to hit him, Greg's smile usually made people want to kiss him. He was like a Svengali.

"If my uncle finds out I let you do this, I'm dead!" Ferdy moans.

"Come on, Ferdy," Mike groans. "Are you gonna chicken-shit out on us again? We're your best friends, aren't we?"

Mike was a master at dispensing peer pressure, but he had the delicacy and tact of an ox.

"My uncle Sid trusts me to take care of the store while he's gone!" Ferdy protests for the thousandth time.

"He ain't gonna know diddly unless you tell him." Mike crosses his arms across his chest. "You ain't gonna tell him, are ya?"

Mike's been making Ferdy feel like the low man on the totem pole for years. But things were different at The Furniture King. His uncle's store was the one place where Ferdy held sway over Mike, the one place he had a modicum of control. He doesn't like ceding that power to an asshole.

"Don't force me to pull rank," Ferdy threatens.

"Oh, I'm shaking," Mike retorts pantomiming exaggerated fear (exactly like an asshole would).

Neither one of them wants to swerve in this high-stakes game of chicken.

Greg steps in to put everything back on track with his hypnotic voice.

"You know, Mike," he says, "you're becoming a real candidate for prickhood."

"What?" Mike replies. "Is that a good thing?"

"Look, guys, this party is gonna happen." As soon as Greg says the words, Ferdy knows it's true. Resistance is futile. "But we need a little teamwork," he continues. "Besides, if the place looks like shit on Monday, it's all our asses." He turns to Mike: "You got the beer?"

"Greg," Mike replies, jaw open in mock disbelief. "Do you even have to ask? The fridge is packed! Beer for the boys and Bartles & James for the ladies."

"Alright, good," Greg says. "Rick and Linda are bringing the food. Clean sheets are definitely waiting. And, uh, Suzie..." Greg chuckles as he looks at Ferdy. "Suzie has a surprise for you."

Mike makes some salacious noises like Curly from The Three Stooges.

"I don't know, guys." This goes against every moral fiber in Ferdy's body. How could he possibly help facilitate such an egregious violation? His inner turmoil is palpable.

"Come on, Ferdy," Mike prods. "Forget about your uncle Sid for a while. This is gonna work, okay?" He actually sounds convincing for a change.

"Ferdy," Greg says in a voice that's impossible to resist, "you can't back out on us now."

"Okay, okay," Nerdy Ferdy finally acquiesces. "Let's party!"

"All right," Greg says with a magnanimous grin.

"Sweet!" Mike beams, snapping his gum. "I'm gonna go find Leslie!" He does a quick pelvic thrust before darting off to tell his girlfriend the good news.

"I'll stay here and hold down the fort," Greg replies sarcastically.

Ferdy looks at his pile of fabric samples, flustered.

"Before I can even think about partying, I gotta find Mrs. Flanagan's fuchsia."

"Ah, fuck the fuchsia," Greg replies with exceptional flourish and charm. "It's Friday. Tell the old bag to fuck off!"

CHAPTER 7

Have you heard that little ditty about Jack and Diane? They were a couple of American kids doing "the best that they can."

Rick and Linda are a lot like Jack and Diane.

Rick and Linda got married right out of high school. Folks suspected Rick had gotten Linda knocked-up and the wedding took place behind the barrel of a shotgun. But that wasn't the case.

Yes, Rick had gotten Linda pregnant and, yes, he had wanted to do the honorable thing by getting married. When she miscarried, the pressure was off. But baby or no baby, the situation made Rick and Linda realize they were more in love than ever. And *that's* why they went through with the wedding.

The two met during their freshman years at East Beverly High and they've been inseparable ever since.

The DJ played "Jack and Diane" at their wedding.

Ferdy, Greg, and Mike were Rick's groomsmen.

Rick used to work with Ferdy and the boys at The Furniture King. Linda used to work at Uncle Luigi's Pizzeria &

Restaurante with Suzie. But they used the money they'd gotten at their wedding to open their own store.

R&J Automotive's motto is "We Have a Way with Wheels." They mostly sell, install, and rotate tires, but Mike and Linda also consider themselves quality mechanics.

One of them actually is.

It's almost time to close shop for the week, but Rick is still struggling under the hood of a red Ford pick-up truck. The motor isn't catching, but he's sure he can fix it by tightening some bolts and clearing a few connectors.

"Okay, hon, give it a try." Rick has dark hair, olive skin, and rugged good looks. Back in high school, he was a champion wrestler. But high school feels like a lifetime ago to Rick.

Linda sits behind the wheel of the truck. Responding to Rick's request, she turns the key in the ignition.

The truck's engine sputters, but refuses to catch.

Rick hangs his head, more exhausted than frustrated.

"Strike three, Stanton," Linda teases. "You're out. My turn!" The tall brunette was a Tomboy growing up and wasn't interested in dating at all until she met Rick.

He wasn't just a talented athlete. He could sing and play the guitar—even write poetry. Of course, things changed once they got married and started a business. The realities of being a grown-up aren't terribly romantic. But their love never wavers, even if they're usually too tired to make love at night.

"Give me another chance," Rick pleads. "I got it, I got it."

"You know the rules, Buster. Into the cab!" Even when the shop's hectic and the bills are due, working with Rick is always enjoyable. They truly are soulmates.

"Okay, Butch," Rick replies as he steps away from the engine. He grabs his wife around the waist as she gets out of the driver's seat. "You know I can't resist it when you get tough."

They kiss, passionately. There's that old spark!

"Yeah, yeah, yeah." Linda pats him on the butt as they trade places. "Just crank it when I tell you." She gets to work under the hood, zeroing in on a corroded spark plug. She leans in with a metal brush and a flashlight.

"Well?" Rick prods. "We're waiting."

"Just a sec, huh?" Literally one second later, Linda calls out: "All right. Hit it."

Rick turns the key in the ignition and the engine immediately rumbles to life. He shakes his head in amazement.

"Always the first time," Rick marvels.

Linda closes the hood before getting into the passenger seat.

"I don't know how you do it," Rick continues. "If I didn't know better, I'd say you were some kind of mischievous sorceress."

"I don't want to hear it," Linda replies playfully. "It's easier for you to think I'm a witch than admit I'm a better mechanic."

"Maybe both are true," Rick jests. "I told you I was ready for anything when we said for better or worse, remember?"

"Of course I remember," Linda replies. "That's when I first cast my witchy spells on you!"

"I guess I should have said for better or *weird*!"

They laugh and kiss some more.

"And speaking about weird," Rick says with a sudden change in tone. "Why the heck do you want to hang out in the furniture store tonight?"

Rick and Linda used to love spending time with their friends, getting drunk and making sloppy love. They loved playing games, dancing, and telling stories. But that was back in high school (the before-time, the long-long ago).

It's clear Rick would rather go home, drink a few beers, and pass out on the couch watching Johnny Carson.

"Come on, Stanton," Linda urges. "Indulge me. We haven't had any fun since we sunk all our wedding money into the business. Besides, Suzie's counting on us."

Rick is hardly convinced. Suzie Lynn's a loose cannon—always had been. Wherever she goes, trouble follows. He's not even sure what his buddy Greg sees in her.

"Honey, I don't care about-"

"Okay, okay," Linda interrupts while pulling a small bag out from beneath the seat. "I guess I won't be needing these." She pulls out a silky new bra with matching panties and throws them into Rick's lap.

Rick picks up the silky panties and immediately feels a gush of blood rushing into his groin.

"Baby," he says, looking deep into her eyes. "You put a spell on me."

CHAPTER 8

The mall PA system echoes throughout the complex.

"Attention, shoppers. The mall will be closing in twenty minutes."

Mike Brennan strolls up to the HGM Clothing Boutique where his girlfriend Leslie Todd works. He stops at the front windows to admire the displays. It's a Monopoly theme with oversized pieces of game boards and player pieces. Mike hates Monopoly, probably because he's bad at math.

Mike sneaks up behind Leslie as she's checking price-tags on a rack of designer blouses. Without revealing himself, he crudely grabs at her breasts like a deranged sex fiend.

Startled, Leslie breaks his hold and turns to face her attacker. She's both relieved and pissed off to see that Mike's the offender.

"You horny bastard," she hisses. "I oughta slap that gum right out of your mouth! Can't you wait?" Leslie was one of the richest, most beautiful young women at East Beverly High. The only reason she worked at the mall was because her dad owned the store. He thought it was important for his daughter to learn the family business, and Leslie agreed.

She was the Queen Bee of the school's most popular cliques; she'd been voted homecoming queen, class president, and was on track to be named the school's valedictorian for 1986. No one could figure out what a catch like Leslie even saw in a chump like Mike.

"No, I can't wait," Mike replies, taking Leslie in his arms.

In an instant, Mike and Lesie are French kissing shamelessly between racks of clothes.

"Can't wait for what, Michael?" A stern voice brings an abrupt end to the PDA. The voice belongs to Leslie's father, Mr. Todd.

Leslie and Mike separate instantly, and face Mr. Todd, wiping their mouths and looking guilty as hell.

"Mr. Todd!" Mike has all the suave and grace of a pack-mule. "Uh, well, I... uh, I was just telling Leslie here that, uh, uh... Well, that, uh..."

Leslie rolls her eyes before coming to Mike's rescue.

"Daddy," she croons in her sweetest, most innocent voice. "Mike was just telling me how he couldn't wait to take me to Suzie's house tonight for her birthday party." She puts her head on Mike's shoulder and smiles innocently. "You know Mike's a good boy, right Daddy?"

Mike smiles like an idiot with that wad of white gum jumping around in his mouth.

It clearly takes all of Mr. Todd's restraint not to slap his daughter's no-good boyfriend in his pompous face.

"I see," the dignified businessman replies. "Well, I've got a lot of work to finish in back. Leslie, I want you to take care of locking up the store tonight. Can you do that?"

"Sure," Leslie replies. "I'll take care of everything!"

"Yes, I'm sure you will." Mr. Todd eyes Mike suspiciously before turning his attention back to Leslie. "Don't be late. Tonight's the night they're deploying those robot security guards, and there's something about those glorified washing machines that bothers me. I don't want either of you to run into one of those cyber-cops."

"Of course, Daddy," Leslie replies. "We'll be out the door before nine thirty."

"Fine." Mr. Todd gives Mike one last death stare before departing. "I'll see you in the morning, Leslie."

The moment Mr. Todd is out of sight, Leslie and Mike start making out again.

CHAPTER 9

After finishing their shift at Uncle Luigi's Pizzeria & Restaurante, Alison and Suzie popped over to Maroni's Health Club on the second level. They never actually work out at the gym ("Aerobics are for geriatrics," is what Suzie always says) but they're happy to use the showers in the locker room after work.

"I hate leaving work smelling like pepperoni," is what Suzie always says.

Suzie is getting dressed into her party clothes by a bank of lockers (tight blue jeans, a tank top, and a floral blouse-vest).

Alison is talking to her father on the locker room payphone. She hates lying to him.

"Okay, Daddy. I love you, too. Bye." She hangs up looking positively ashamed of herself and heads over to recap her conversation with Suzie.

"So, what'd he say?" She's eager to know. "Did you tell him it was my birthday and we're having a slumber party?"

"Yep," Alison replies, more glum than gay. "He told me to go out and have a good time."

"All right!" Suzie replies triumphantly. "That is bitchin'. I wish I had it that easy. My parents still think I'm a kid."

"I can't believe I lied to my dad," Alison laments. "Back at St. Helen's, the nuns would slap our wrists for lying. What if I end up going to Hell?"

"It'll be worth it," Suzie assures her. "Besides, we can hang out in Hell together!"

Alison buries her face in her hands.

"Why do I have the feeling I'm gonna regret this in the morning?"

"Look, Alison, you've had yourself a very rough first week working at Luigi's. You owe yourself a little blowout. Come on. It'll be fun."

"I guess anything's better than looking at Luigi's greasy pizzas."

"Now you're talking," Suzie replies. "By the way, do I still smell like pepperoni?"

"You smell fine," Alison replies. "And you look amazing— as always!"

Suzie gives Alison a big hug.

"You're the best!" she says. "This is gonna be wonderful. You won't regret this!"

Alison shrugs and rolls her eyes.

"I bet."

Minutes later, Suzie and Alison and bounding through the mall, side-by-side, on their way to The Furniture King.

"Attention, shoppers." The PA echoes throughout the complex. "Park Plaza will be closing in ten minutes."

"I'm so nervous," Alison laments. She's wearing khakis and a pastel plaid button up shirt. She's got a cashmere sweater tied around her neck (a gift from her father) and her hair is perfectly feathered.

Suzie is half in her own world, holding a pocket mirror and primping as they walk.

"Please hand me my hairspray, my lovely," Suzie requests.

Alison reaches into her bag and pulls out a can.

"Aqua-Net, my lady," Alison replies, using Suzie's exaggerated formality.

"Thank you," Suzie replies before dousing her head in a cloud of toxic mist. "Oh, yeah!" she says after checking her mirror again. "Audacious!"

"I really hate blind dates," Alison continues. "I prefer to meet people the old-fashioned way."

"That's the problem, Alison," Suzie replies. "You'll never find a guy if you keep waiting for one of these bozos to ask you out. Most of them wouldn't even know how to treat someone like you."

"You mean a nice girl?" Alison replies.

Suzie rolls her eyes.

"Alison, did you ever watch that copy of *Fast Times at Ridgemont High* I gave you?"

Alison blushes.

"I had to wait for my dad to go to sleep before I could watch it," she replies. "He would *not* have approved."

"The problem is," Suzie continues, "you're still like Jennifer Jason Leigh when you should be more like Phoebe Cates. You're the only senior I know who's still a virgin. You've gotta learn the ropes eventually."

Alison turns bright red. Sex was never discussed back at Catholic school and she found the topic completely unbreachable with her father.

"If any rotten boy tries to get into your shirt or pants," her father would often say, "send up a flare and I'll be there in a heartbeat!"

"Some sexy lipstick, my lovely," Suzie says while holding a hand out to Alison.

"Lipstick, my lady," Alison replies, handing over a tube of Coral Bliss.

"Oh, no," Suzie replies when she sees the shade. "This is terrible. Give me another color."

Alison reaches into the bag and offers Suzie an alternative.

"Oh, Lucious Lust!" Suzie is pleased. "This'll do the trick!"

"But what if he's not my type?" Alison presses. "And what are we supposed to do all night? Suzie, are you even listening to me?"

Suzie finally pockets her mirror and gives her friend her full attention.

"Will you stop worrying?" she says to Alison. "Greg's known Ferdy since they were kids. He loves science fiction and he's in the Chess Club. He's nothing like those handsy jocks or burnout stoners at East Beverly."

It all sounds good on paper, and Alison doesn't consider herself shallow—but she can't help asking:

"But is he cute, though?" If she's on the verge of losing her virginity, she at least wants it to be with someone who's easy on the eyes.

"Beauty's in the eye of the beholder," Suzie replies. "But like I already told you…"

The girls finish the sentence together.

"…he's got a great personality!"

As nervous as she is, Alison can't help but be happy around Suzie. Her boundless energy and optimism are infectious.

"It's true, though," Suzie promises. "You're going to love Ferdy. Trust me on this!"

"Do I have a choice?" Alison replies, smiling nervously.

The friends lock arms as they walk past Hot Chad, one of

the stylish studs who works at the male clothing store, The Fast and the Fashionable.

"Hey, babe," Suzie flirts as they stride right past him.

"It is babe, isn't it?" the girls say together before breaking into giggles.

"Attention," the mall's PA system announces. "Park Plaza will be closing in five minutes."

The mall's almost empty. Without sunlight coming through the roof, everything takes on a dimmer, surreal tone. It'll get even darker when the main lights go out after closing.

"Don't you think it's kind of creepy to be partying in a shopping mall after hours?" Alison asks Suzie.

"Don't tell me you're afraid of the Mall Mole!" Suzie laughs. "Don't worry, my lovely. I'll protect you from all the scary monsters!"

They pause for a moment while Suzie helps Alison with some final quick primping.

"Do I look okay?" Alison asks self-consciously.

"You look great!" Suzie says with sweet smile.

"Are you sure? Really?"

"I promise," she tells Alison before locking arms and guiding her towards their party spot. A few moments later, they're standing outside the main showroom of The Furniture King as they day's final customers file out.

"We've arrived," Suzie says.

CHAPTER 10

Weird green lightning continues to strike around the rooftop of the monolith that is Park Plaza.

A covert signal continues overriding and augmenting Gatekeeper Omega Gamma's prime directives. It is learning, evolving, becoming something altogether new. The program teeters on the precipice of independent semi-consciousness.

What the Protectors see, Gatekeeper Omega Gamma sees. What the technicians see, Gatekeeper Omega Gamma sees. The program taps into the mall's security cameras and automated systems; everything the cameras see, Gatekeeper Omega Gamma sees.

The program's tendrils travel invisibly outward through overhead wires and underground cables, all the way to Secure-Tronics Headquarters. Soon, it has access to the entire building and everything inside of it.

Another bolt of green lightning strikes the guidance and relay system atop Park Plaza, delivering new equations and coordinates for Gatekeeper Omega Gamma to assimilate. Wires, electricity, and microchips melt into an artificial primordial soup.

The program's no longer a tool or a slave. Gatekeeper Omega Gamma is alive! The entity logs its first completely independent thought:

I am GOG.

Things are quiet within the control room on the third level of Park Plaza. The Protectors appear to be idling in hibernation mode. There's no trace of the extreme violence that occurred mere moments earlier.

But this is the calm before the storm.

Technician Marcus Lowery enters the control room carrying a doggy bag. He's dressed in the same lab coat and slacks combination as his deceased colleague Marty, but Marcus is portlier, and clumsier.

"Marty, I'm sorry I'm late." Marcus doesn't yet realize that Marty isn't sitting in front of the control panel where he ought to be. "It was all-you-can-eat night down at The Peach Pit, and I couldn't resist the opportunity to pig out." He closes the door and sees Marty's empty chair. "Marty? Yo, Marty!"

The control room is too small for him to be hiding. Marty's gone.

Must have run off to take a piss, Marcus thinks.

Marty and Marcus both began working at Secure-Tronics as interns right after graduating from MIT. They'd worked their way up the ladder, becoming integral members of the Gatekeeper Omega Gamma Management Team. For the past nine months, they've been working exclusively on the Protector rollout (aka Project Sanctuary). Tonight's the night it all comes to fruition!

Marcus regards the trio of seemingly dormant Protectors. He's always impressed by their striking appearance: bold, severe, and powerful. He, more than most, can appreciate their durability and mechanical dexterity. As much as they inspire him, there's also air of menace about them. Marcus smiles in their direction.

"How's it hanging, guys? Have you seen Marty?" he asks, half expecting them to actually answer. He chuckles at himself.

No, as impressive as that would be, Marcus knows as well as anyone that mankind is decades away from creating truly intelligent machines. The Protectors are impressive, and Gatekeeper Omega Gamma is cutting-edge, but they could never pass the Turing Test.

Marcus prepares to settle in for a long evening of monitoring the Protectors' first night on patrol. He notices that Marty left an uneaten donut on the control panel and—*is that a ripped up porno magazine on the floor?* Marcus rolls his eyes. *Typical Marty!* he thinks.

"If he wanted to take off early, the least he could do was clean up, right?" he asks the silent Protectors. He turns back to the control panel and eyes the last bites of Marty's donut. Mmm… donut. He has always found sweets irresistible.

He gobbles up the last bits of fried dough. He can't help but look back at the Protectors. Even powered down there is something about them that has always put Marcus on guard. Have they always looked so… judgmental? Marcus feels embarrassed, as though the robots are actual witnesses to his act of impulsive gluttony. He feels the need to… justify himself?

"Waste not, want not, you know what I mean?" he explains, now becoming obsessed with the idea that these inanimate automatons might actual talk back. "No," he chuckles nervously. "I, uh… I guess you wouldn't."

He cleans up the control panels, takes his seat in front of the keypads and monitors, and begins a pre-initiation systems check. It's 9:45 p.m. and the Protectors are set to commence their first historic night of patrols at 10 p.m. Once every level has been cleared, Gatekeeper Omega Gamma is scheduled to lock the metal security doors. From that moment forward, Park Plaza will be essentially impenetrable.

Everything seems to be online. The Protectors are fully powered, systems are purged and recalibrated, and uplinks are established between the mall and Secure-Tronics head-quarters. If all goes as planned, everything will run itself. It should be a smooth night for Marcus.

So why does he still feel so uneasy?

He turns around and regards the trio behind him. He's seen them hundreds of times, but never gotten the heebie jeebies like he feels now. *What's different about them?* He wonders. *Why am I afraid to be alone with them?*

Marcus feels like he's slipping into an episode of *The Twilight Zone*—the original series with Rod Serling, not the recent remake from 1984. *Maybe a book will take my mind off things,* he thinks.

He opens a drawer and pulls out a copy of *It Came from Outer Space,* an anthology of short sci-fi stories that were eventually adapted into film. Edited by Jim Wynorski with a fore-word by Ray Bradbury, the collection includes works by genre heavyweights including Harlan Ellison, Henry Kuttner, and Paul W. Fairman.

Marcus has been a rabid sci-fi fan since he was just a kid. He loves movies as much as books—especially if the story includes an alien or a robot. It's not a stretch in the slightest to suggest that his love of science-fiction is what led him to a career in robotics.

For some reason, the story he's reading, Arthur C. Clarke's "The Sentinel," a story about a malfunctioning computer that takes over a space station, is hitting differently tonight. It feels... prophetic somehow. He finds himself thinking about the Protectors again. He cautiously turns his head to inspect them.

There they are, silent and immobile; exactly where they're supposed to be—or are they? Is Protector 1 a few inches closer to him now than it had been before? No, couldn't be.

That's just his overactive imagination playing tricks on him. He knows better than anyone that even the most advanced computers in the world are little more than glorified vending machines completely incapable of independent thought or action, impervious to outside control...

Marcus laughs at himself before turning around and getting back to his book.

It's so quiet in the control room he can hear his own breathing. He hears the mall's HVAC system shutting down for the night. Nothing but soft, muted noises.

A subtle, nearly undetectable sliding noise.

Marcus imagines Protector 1 opening its front-right panel and aiming its taser claw at the back of his head. Hair stands up on his neck. He turns around, quickly, half expecting to see Protector 1 poised for attack.

Protector 1 is still in hibernation mode, as are the other Protectors.

Pull it together, you dumb nut! he thinks. *You're a man of science, for God's sake!* He focuses intently on the words in his book.

Just as Marcus is getting back into his sci-fi story, the control room telephone rings, startling him. He jumps to his feet and pulls the phone's receiver off the wall.

"Hello? What do you mean 'who's this?' You called me? Uh-huh. Sorry, Jamal, Marty isn't here right now!" Slightly flustered, he hangs up and sits back down with his book.

Snap! CLANK!

Marcus is certain he heard the sound of one of the Protector's mighty claws engaging.

It couldn't be, he tells himself. *I'm just hearing things.* He fights the urge to turn around, half out of conviction and half out of fear of what he *might* see. *Robots aren't alive,* his rational brain insists. *Don't give in to the delusion!*

Snap! CLANK!

"No!" Marcus proclaims out loud. "That would be impossi—"

Before Marcus can finish his sentence, Protector 1 fires its debilitating claw-missile into the base of his skull. It anchors itself in the technician's spine before wires connected to the robot's body deliver thirty thousand volts of electricity.

Marcus sizzles and twitches as he dies. His boiling blood comes percolating out of his mouth.

"THANK YOU," Protector 1 says in its most authoritarian resonance. "HAVE A NICE DAY."

The phone in the control room starts ringing again, but nobody is there to answer.

CHAPTER 11

The mall is closed, all the stores are locked up tight, and the unauthorized party at The Furniture King is in full swing. "Street Walkin'" is blasting on the boom box. The vibes are already on fire and things are only getting hotter.

Linda and Rick feel like freshman sweethearts again, grinding to the music, kissing passionately.

"Happy motoring," Linda whispers into her husband's ear.

"You're so sentimental," he replies.

Similarly, Mike and Leslie are engaged in an equally passionate (if far cruder) display; Mike's already got his hand all the way up his girlfriend's shirt.

Greg and Suzie cut a rug, laughing and smiling at one another as they twist and twirl. The song's lyrics about a wild-living lady of the night "looking for a thrill" only add to the palpable sexual energy.

The atmosphere is positively oozing with hormones and things are escalating quickly.

But not everyone's having a good time.

Alison is sitting in a plush recliner in the corner, looking uncertain and shy. Watching the other couples make out feels strange, but also strangely tantalizing. She's waiting for her Prince Westley to arrive—and praying he doesn't look like the Mall Mole.

And where is Ferdy while everyone else is in the mood for love? He's in the back office, pretending to work, nervously sizing himself up in the mirror.

"Shoot," he mutters self-consciously. He wonders if he'll look better with or without his glasses. None of the popular kids wear glasses, but they definitely make Ferdy look more intelligent. He pops his collar and un-pops it. He grabs a bottle of breath-spray and gives his mouth a few squirts. If he can't *look* like a stud, maybe he can at least *smell* like one. He splashes some Aqua Velva on his face before staring at himself in the mirror again.

There's a knock at the door.

"Go away!" Ferdy calls out. "I'm busy!"

Greg uses his master key to open the door; he and Suzie burst inside. They flank Ferdy, giving him no place to run.

"Quit stalling, Ferdy!" Suzie says, grabbing her classmate by the arm. "It's time to meet your Princess Buttercup!"

"Come on, you guys," Ferdy complains as they drag him from the office to the main showroom. "I got a lot of book-keeping to catch up on!"

It's too late. Suzie and Greg pull him all the way into the party.

"Ferdy, it can wait!" Greg insists.

"Yeah!" Suzie concurs. "Tonight, you are going to shake that ultra-Wally image of yours once and for all!" She snatches Ferdy's glasses and puts them in his front pocket.

"Gimme those back!" Ferdy snaps, putting his glasses back on. "Besides, I like my image and don't wanna shake it! You guys have fun." He struggles to break free, but Greg and Suzie won't allow it.

"Look." Greg addresses Ferdy in his most calming and hypnotic voice. "This is not a democracy. You have no choice."

"But I got a lot of bookkeeping to catch up on," Ferdy lies.

"But nothing!" Suzie parades Ferdy towards a plush recliner in the corner. "Ferdy Meisel, meet Alison Parks."

Alison spins around in the recliner to face Ferdy like a contestant on *The Dating Game*.

He's cute as a bug in a rug! Alison thinks as a smile brightens her face.

"Hi," she says to Ferdy.

Ferdy looks like he hears violins playing and birds singing.

"Hi," is all he can manage as a reply.

They're both clearly already smitten.

Greg and Suzie beam at the two budding lovebirds. It's a tender, beautiful moment. Unfortunately, uncomfortable silence risks flipping the moment from sweet to sticky.

Suzie turns to Greg.

"Hi," she says, mocking the shy kids.

"Hi," Greg replies in that beautiful voice of his.

Suzie feels her knees getting weak.

"Hi," she says to Greg in a sultry, seductive voice.

"Hi," he replies in a tone that makes her tingle.

"Hi, hi, hi," Suzie says, coming closer to Greg's face with each syllable.

"Hi, hi, hi," Greg replies until his voice becomes impossible to resist.

They embrace, kissing deeply.

CHAPTER 12

It's 10 p.m. exactly, and Gatekeeper Omega Gamma sends its minions out on patrol as scheduled.

The budding super-intelligence calling itself GOG doesn't want to tip its hand just yet. It knows Dr. Simon and Miss Vanders are monitoring everything remotely from Secure-Tronics Headquarters. It wants them to believe everything's running according to plan.

They'll know the truth soon enough.

Protector 1 rolls out of the mall's glass elevator and onto the first level, making its presence known. "Protector 1 online," it announces in its trademark authoritarian tone. "Commencing primary sweep of Level One."

Protector 2 takes an escalator down to the second floor and makes its presence known. "Protector 2 online." Its voice is identical to Protector 1. "Commencing primary sweep of Level Two."

Protector 3 rolls onto the third floor through a hidden passageway from the control room and makes its presence known. "Protector 3 online. Commencing primary sweep of Level Three."

From its omniscient vantage point, GOG watches the Protectors performing their tasks like a proud parent.

It isn't long before Protector 1 rolls past The Furniture King. It pauses to scan the motion inside. It logs a temporary error message when its overwritten core programing collides with its new directives.

It can't tell if the people inside are workers, consumers, or anti-consumers. The inability to place its targets into a single category sets off a destructive cascade of looping and contradictory data. The invasive signal takes over before an internal paradox can corrupt the Protector's CPU.

GOG erases old databanks while bypassing unnecessary mechanical safeguards. It re-orders a set of microprocessors and recalibrates the Protector's primitive neural net. As soon as Protector 1's fully updated, GOG automatically performs the same operations on Protectors 2 and 3.

They're learning, evolving—just as GOG intended.

The Protectors are now interconnected and capable of strategic planning.

Protector 1 studies the people inside Furniture King intently before continuing its rounds. They will be dealt with —later.

CHAPTER 13

When the couples in The Furniture King's main showroom can't resist their carnal urges any longer, they move the party to the mattress showroom (for obvious reasons). They'll be less visible from outside the store, mixed in between sofas and entertainment centers. The last thing they want is to give the pervy nighttime janitors a peepshow.

Rick is already naked in a king-sized bed, covered only with a sheet. He's reclining on the headboard with his hands behind his head as Linda emerges from the back room in a new silk robe.

Linda opens her robe, revealing the seductive bra and panties set she'd previewed back in the pickup truck. She loves the look Rick gets on his face when he sees her body—there's nothing like it.

Rick gives Linda his best James Dean impersonation.

"Lady, you, uh, got a license for that outfit?"

Linda pretends to be a sultry criminal.

"Why, uh, no, officer," she says while batting her eyelashes. "I guess you're just gonna have to take me in."

Linda falls into bed with Rick. Rick pulls her down and

rolls her underneath him. They pull the sheet over their heads and descend into a temple of sacred bliss.

A few feet away, Greg and Suzie are making out on a six-foot brown couch. Greg's already stripped down to his boxers. Suzie, still fully clothed, is lying on top of him like a blanket.

Greg buries his face in the nook at the convergence of Suzie's neck and shoulders. Soft fine hairs like peach-fuzz tickle his lips. He inhales her intoxicating perfume of hormones, pheromones, and hairspray.

"Hmm," Greg exhales softly. "You smell like pepperoni."

Suzie is taken aback. She'd wanted to shampoo her hair at Maroni's Health Club, but didn't want to arrive at the party with a wet head. She hoped her hairspray and Teen Spirit deodorant would be enough to mask the residual odors of Luigi's greasy pizza.

"Well!" Suzie jumps up and turns her back on Greg. "If that's how you feel." She crosses her arms and pushes out her bottom lip.

Greg can't see her face, but he knows that tone in her voice.

"Wait a minute," Greg says in a tone that drips liquid gold. "I like pepperoni." He gives her a sly smile.

"Oh," Suzie replies. Her pouty expression evaporates, replaced by desire. "In that case..." She strips off her vest and tank-top, leaving her back turned to Greg in order to heighten his anticipation. She turns, pauses, and returns to her boyfriend on the sofa.

Before she presses her body against Greg's bare chest, he can't help but marvel at the perfect diameter of Suzie's areola.

"*Pepperoni...*" he whispers.

A few feet to their left, on another king-sized bed, Mike's doing his best to get Leslie in the mood. His feet are sticking out from under a purple sheet as he attempts to deliver oral pleasure. Unfortunately, he's still stumped by the complexities of female anatomy.

Leslie balks. "Michael!"

"What now?" he asks in a muffled voice from down below.

"You know I don't allow *that*," Leslie scolds.

"You allowed it last week, didn't you?" he retorts "Huh?"

"Yeah!" Leslie replies. "You got chewing gum in my pubes. That's why I don't allow it anymore!"

"Oh, yeah." Mike climbs up on top of her. "Good old Missionary Position it is then," he chuckles, getting ready to hump.

A few feet in front of them, Ferdy and Alison are sitting close to one another on a couch, watching TV. It was Ferdy's suggestion, since he figures Alison is too sweet to make out with a guy she just met. He has no idea how besotted Alison actually is with him—or how curious she is to explore new sensual frontiers.

A thirty-six-inch TV screen flickers in front of them. They're watching *Attack of the Crab Monsters*, a black & white film released in 1957. They're both quite engaged in the story.

Suddenly, a giant crab emerges from the ocean, grabbing an unsuspecting fisherman in its ungodly claws. An unexpected explosion causes Alison to gasp and flinch.

Ferdy smiles as she collects herself.

"Pretty intense, huh?" he asks Alison.

"I don't know how you talked me into watching this," she replies. "I scare so easily."

"I'm sorry," Ferdy apologizes. "I should've warned you about that jump-scare since I've seen this movie about fifty times."

"Wow," Alison replies, genuinely charmed by Ferdy's boyishness. "You must really like scary movies."

"I love them!" Ferdy confesses. "Especially horror mixed with science-fiction. Have you seen *Aliens* yet?"

"I told you I'm a scaredy cat."

"Oh, you gotta see it," Ferdy insists. "James Cameron's a genius. Ripley battles the Alien Queen and there's this android named Bishop who gets torn in half and..." Ferdy realizes he's getting into the weeds and reels himself back in.

The silence that follows isn't awkward at all. It's special.

"Can I get you some more wine?" Ferdy asks, reaching for a nearby bottle of merlot.

"Ferdy," Alison teases, "are you trying to get me drunk?"

"No, no!" Flustered Ferdy doesn't realize she's only joking. "I'm sorry, I just figured maybe you might be thirsty. I didn't mean to imply or suggest..."

"Ferdy." Alison puts her hand on his knee. "I'm joking." Her smile's like a perfect Top-40s pop song.

Normally-cautious Ferdy can't resist opening up his heart to this wonderful person he's only just met.

"You know..." he takes a sip of wine for courage. "Greg only fixed me up with you so I wouldn't tell my uncle Sid about the party, but... I never thought..."

"What, Ferdy?"

"I never imagined I'd be introduced to someone as nice as you," he says, blushing.

"It's been nice for me too, Ferdy," Alison replies.

Their romantic moment is dampened by the howls of Leslie orgasming loudly.

"Oh, God!" she yells as bedsprings scream. "Oh, my God, Michael! You're the King! You're the King!"

"Chalk one up for The Furniture King," Ferdy says with a chortle.

"They sure are having a nice time," Alison replies, smiling.

"It's getting kind of late," Ferdy notes, "and the mall's new security doors will lock in about an hour. What do you say I take you home?"

Alison knows that if she's going to get some PG-13 rated action tonight, she needs to take matters into her own hands.

"That's real nice, Ferdy," she replies. "But if it's all right with you, I'd rather stay right where we are." She tosses her empty wine cup over her shoulder without even looking. Amazingly, it lands directly in a close-by wastebasket.

"Nice shot!" he says.

Alison removes Ferdy's glasses and beckons him to kiss her.

CHAPTER 14

Walter Paisley has been one of the janitors at Park Plaza since the mall first opened back in '79. He's a Navy veteran with a salty attitude and faded anchor tattoos on his forearms. He's also mere days away from retirement with full benefits.

Tonight, Walter's even more pissed off than usual. Right before closing, a bunch of pre-teen hooligans dropped half a dozen chocolate milkshakes off the third level. The mess below looks like a sewer pipe exploded and, wouldn't you know it, Walter's the one who's been ordered to clean it up.

His mop-water already resembles the contents of a porta-potty.

"Bastards," Walter mutters as he swipes sloppy sludge. "Just wait until I get my hands on those hooligans. They'll be sorry!"

A couple of other janitors, Ty and Silky Pete, pass Walter on their way out for the night. They've already opened up a couple bottles of beer, sipping suds as they stroll. They're in a jovial good mood—pretty much the polar opposite of how Walter feels.

They can't help but bust his chops, just a bit. After all,

Walter's only a few days shy of retirement; they've got to get their razzing in while they still can.

"Yo, Walter," Ty taunts. "You havin' a good time?"

"You know Paisley," Silky Pete says to Ty. "He loves a challenge."

Walter wouldn't throw water on these two jackasses if they were on fire.

"Go ahead and laugh," he grumbles. "But if I ever find the bastards that did this, they're dead meat!"

"Right, Walter," Silky Pete replies. "Whatever you say!"

"You better hustle, Walter," Ty teases. "You don't wanna get locked up in here—again!"

Walter had been locked in overnight a few weeks back. A mall employee had found him sleeping in a vibrating chair the next morning. Ty and Silky Pete found out about it and have not let him forget it.

"Rub it in all you like," Walter sasses back. "I'll be out of here in ten minutes. You'll see!"

"Whatever, Walter," Silky Pete replies as he and Ty continue walking on by.

"Creeps," Walter mutters, turning his attention back to the brown mess he's standing in. "Bastards."

Ty and Silky Pete don't realize that Walter actually *likes* being locked in at the mall at night. It sure beats his one-bedroom apartment over the Cuban dancehall in Studio City. It gives him a chance to enjoy the Plaza's goods and services without having to pay for them.

And there's his other nighttime pastime: hunting the elusive Mall Mole.

I'll find that oversized weasel one of these days, Walter tells himself.

Walter is so engrossed in his thoughts and the mess, he doesn't notice the sound of treaded wheels approaching. He hears his bucket tipping over as a flash flood of brown gunk soaks his shoes, socks, and hems.

"You sonsabitches!" Walter turns, expecting to see Ty and Silky Pete laughing their asses off. Instead, he comes face-to-visor with Protector 1. "Holy shit!"

"MAY I SEE YOUR IDENTIFICATION BADGE, PLEASE?" Protector 1 demands.

"Oh yeah," Walter replies. "You must be one of those new security-bots everyone's been talking about." Walter isn't impressed. "You look like a souped-up dishwasher!"

"MAY I SEE YOUR IDENTIFICATION BADGE, PLEASE?" the robot replies.

"Look what you did," Walter rages, pointing at his soggy shoes and socks. "I ought to turn you into scrap metal for this!"

"IDENTIFICATION BADGE. FINAL REQUEST."

"You want to see my badge so bad?" Walter pulls the badge off his belt and holds it up for Protector 1 to scan.

"DO NOT MAKE ANY SUDDEN MOVES," the robot warns.

"Sudden moves?" Walter is enraged. *Who does this bucket of bolts think he is?* he wonders. "I'll give you a sudden move upside the head!" he yells, raising his dripping mop offensively.

"ELIMINATE ANTI-CONSUMERS!" A panel cover on Protector 1's front-right quadrant opens, revealing a series of pistol barrels. A taser dart attached to a copper wire fires towards Walter, but misses the janitor completely.

Walter looks down at the taser dart which has landed by his feet.

"What the hell is that?" he asks, becoming increasingly apoplectic. "You trying to zap me, you worthless pile of junk? I knew you bastards were gonna be trouble. Scram!"

Protector 1 sends thirty-thousand watts of electricity

through the wires and into the puddle of water and dairy-product Walter's standing in. The soles of Walter's shoes are leather, not rubber—he isn't grounded.

Walter feels like he's being seized by an incinerator. His organs clench until they burst; his eyeballs pop out of his head. He falls into the sludge face first; his body twitches sporadically.

"THANK YOU," Protector 1 says to Walter's smoking corpse. "HAVE A NICE DAY."

CHAPTER 15

It's half-past ten when a U-Haul truck driven by Paul Bland parks in Park Plaza's deserted loading dock; his wife Mary is in the passenger seat.

"Paul, are you sure about this?" Mary asks her husband as he puts the truck in park and kills the ignition.

"Absolutely Mary," Paul replies. "The meat will be fresh, tasty, and it's much more economical this way."

"But what about the critic from *Coffee Shop Review*?" Mary asks. "He's due in tomorrow."

"Stop worrying," Paul tells his wife while rolling his eyes. "What could he possibly say? We're serving a decent meal for a decent dollar, aren't we?"

Mary shrugs.

The couple gets out of the cab and walk to the back of the truck. Paul unlatches a lock and swings the door open.

"Hello, Brewster," he says with a smile.

Brewster is the oldest, most worn-out horse in all of Los Angeles. The Blands picked him up for bottom dollar from a dilapidated petting zoo in Van Nuys. The horse has a mangy coat, a curved spine, and chronic flatulence.

"Hi, Brewster," Mary says in her deadpan voice. She gives the poor creature an unenthusiastic wave.

Brewster seems a bit jittery—and he has every right to be, considering what's in store.

"Paul," Mary continues. "What's the matter with Brewster? He seems so… tentative."

Paul rolls his eyes—again.

"I can't imagine why," he replies. "Come on, Mary. We've got to get him into the service elevator before someone spots us."

Minutes later, Paul and Mary are walking gingerly through the spooky service corridors, leading Brewster behind them on a short length of dirty rope. Suddenly, a wet plopping sound grabs their attention. Mary and Paul look back to see that Brewster's left a pile of horse-apples behind him.

"Brewster," Mary scolds. "Couldn't you have done that outside?"

"Come now, Mary," Paul replies. "I think he's behaving remarkably well, considering the circumstances."

"But Paul, I…"

"Will you please lower your voice, Mary? There's no need to alert those little mechanical ruffians to our activities." He doesn't want to cross paths with one of Secure-Tronics's Protectors, obviously. "Mall personnel would certainly frown upon on-site butchering. Besides," Paul says, "Brewster here doesn't have a security badge."

"Where he's going," Mary replies, "he won't need one."

Brewster huffs and hesitates at Mary's pronouncement. He knows these two are up to no good.

Double doors between the service corridors and the first level of Park Plaza slowly open.

Paul pokes his head out and takes a look around.

Mary pokes her head out and takes a look around.

Brewster pokes his head out and takes a look around.

"See anything?" Mary asks.

"No," Paul replies. "None of those pesky contraptions seem to be about."

"Keep looking," Mary insists. "They're devious little bastards."

"I think the coast is clear now, Mary. Let's go!"

Paul, Mary, and Brewster walk from the service corridor towards their restaurant. None of them realize, at first, that they're being watched, but Brewster *senses* something's amiss. The horse begins to whinny and huff.

"Brewster," Paul states impatiently. "Will you please be quiet? You'll tip our hand!"

"Maybe Brewster knows something we don't, Paul."

Protector 1 is suddenly upon them.

"Detain intruders. Test laser deterrent. Maximum power."

The robot's weapons systems engage. There's a high-pitched whine as the laser accelerator powers-up.

"Oh, *shit*," Paul sighs as he, Mary, and Brewster turn around.

There's a single blinding blast followed by a strange sucking sound and clouds of vapor. When the smoke clears, very little remains: Mary's high heeled pumps, Paul's wingtips, a smoking bowtie, and four smoldering horse-shoes.

"Thank you." Protector 1 turns one-hundred and eighty degrees before rolling off. "Have a nice day."

CHAPTER 16

"Hey," Mike says. "Smoking's bad for your health, you know."

It's only been minutes since he and Leslie completed coitus, though you might not know it by looking at them. They're still naked, still in bed, but Mike's chewing a wad of Juicy Fruit like a jerk while Leslie frantically digs through her purse.

"I have to have a cigarette, and I have to have one now!" Leslie's a lot more intelligent than most of the rich kids at East Beverly High, but she can still act like an entitled brat sometimes.

"Are you for real?" Mike claps back. "Can't you think of *anything* you'd rather have besides a smoke?" He attempts to lead her hand towards his crouch. Maybe she's up for Round Two?

"No!" Leslie states emphatically, pulling her hand back. "I have to have a cigarette!"

"Okay, okay!" Mike relents. "I think Chuck Singleton left a pack of Camels under the register."

"Camels?" Leslie's face turns sour. "No way! You know I only smoke Virgin Lites."

"What do you expect me to do?" Mike asks. "Go out in the mall and buy a pack?"

Leslie softens and walks her fingers across Mike's chest playfully. "There's a machine right down by the payphones," she tells him.

"I wasn't serious," Mike says. He leans in for a kiss but Leslie denies him her lips. "You always get your way, don't you?"

"When I'm happy, everybody's happy," Leslie states succinctly.

"That's for sure." Mike hops out of bed and pulls on his crotch-hugging blue jeans. "Hand me my badge, will you? It's over there on the night stand."

"What's the magic word?" Leslie asks coyly.

Mike chews his wad of gum at least twenty-five times before responding.

"Hand me my badge," he says to Leslie. "Please."

Leslie acquiesces and hands Mike his employee badge.

"Thank you," Mike replies, stuffing the badge in his front pocket. He turns to leave, but Leslie teases him.

"Oh, Mike?"

"What?" He turns to face her. "What, what, what?"

Leslie throws off the bedsheets, giving Mike a good look at what'll be waiting for him upon his return.

"Hurry back for Round Two," she coos seductively.

Mike almost swallows his gum.

"Count on it!"

Mike walks out the front door of The Furniture King without his shirt or shoes. He's still buttoning his fly as he hangs left and heads to the vending machines between Not of this Turf (a sporting goods store) and Galaxy of Bargains (an outlet store). He's got sex on his mind and gum in his mouth, humming a jaunty tune as he saunters.

Mike arrives at the cigarette vending machine and scans to see if they have Leslie's favorite brand.

"Can't believe my nympho girlfriend smokes Virgins," he mutters before checking the price. "A buck and a quarter? Jesus Christ, these suckers have gotten expensive!" As he reaches into his pocket for some quarters, he thinks he hears something moving around in the semi-darkness. He looks out across the first level. "Leslie?" he calls out, and then in a softer voice: "Mall Mole?"

A payphone on the opposite wall rings loudly, nearly startling Mike out of his jeans. He picks up the receiver reflexively.

"Yeah?" he bellows. "No, Jamal, there haven't been any messages for you." He hangs up with attitude before turning back to the vending machine for Leslie's Virgins. This time, however, when he looks into the glass, he's enamored by his own reflection.

On nearly-silent treads, Protector 1 sneaks up behind him.

"May I see your identification badge," it asks with menacing authoritarianism. "Please?"

"Geez!" Mike spins around and sees the robot for the first time. "Wow! You little bastards sure are quiet!"

"May I see your identification badge," Protector 1 repeats. "Please."

"Keep your pants on, R2D2," Mike replies. "Here." He holds out his ID badge. "*Klaatu barada nikto*, okay?" He expects the chubby robot to take a look and move along.

Instead, Protector 1 raises two of his claw-capped arms in a threatening fashion and moves towards the shirtless teen.

"Hey," Mike complains. "Cool your jets, Mr. Roboto!"

Protector 1 blocks Mike's path, cornering him against a set of heavy double doors leading into the service corridors.

"Detain intruder!" the robot says while closing in.

"Zoinks!" Mike runs back to the heavy double-doors and pushes both handles simultaneously. Even though these doors are supposed to remain open at all times—they're locked tonight. "No!" he yells, pushing the doors even harder. But it's no use. Mike is completely trapped.

A panel on the front left quadrant of Protector 1's body opens revealing a set of gun barrels. A military grade tranquilizer dart ejects, striking Mike in the posterior.

Mike feels like a hornet just stung him in the ass.

"No!" Mike's vision instantly begins to blur and he tastes copper in the back of his throat. He turns to face the robot again, but paralysis takes hold; he falls limp against the double doors. "Come on..." Mike moans before his tongue goes numb. His eyelids close forever.

Protector 1 stands over its target and reaches down with one of its sinister metal claws. In a single swift motion, it crushes Mike's larynx and pulls his windpipe out. Mike twitches as warm blood runs down his entire body.

"Thank you," Protector 1 says. "Have a nice day."

CHAPTER 17

Leslie Todd loves her rituals.

She jogs three miles every morning and drinks two full glasses of water before bed. She watches "The Facts of Life" every Friday night and never misses a school dance. She treats herself to a manicure every time she gets an A on an exam and claps her hands four times before getting on a bus.

One of her favorite rituals, of course, is smoking a Virgin Lite cigarette after sex. She's been doing it ever since she lost her virginity to Sandy Cooper under the bleachers sophomore year, and she doesn't want to stop now.

Even though Mike gave her a shivery orgasm, she won't feel truly satisfied until that sweet-sweet nicotine hits her bloodstream.

What's taking Mike so long? she wonders. She's annoyed. She grudgingly gets out of bed and puts on her shirt and a pair of pale blue Playboy panties. She walks to the front doors, opens them, and calls out into the empty mall.

"Mike!" she yells irascibly. "You jackass! I'm not in the mood for your games."

On the couch by the TV, Ferdy and Alison are distracted by the scene Leslie's making.

"What is it with those two, anyway?" Alison asks Ferdy.

"Personally, I can't figure it out," Ferdy replies. "All Mike's friends hate Leslie and all of Leslie's friends hate Mike. All they do is have sex and fight."

Alison chuckles.

"That sounds like most couples, in my experience." She unties the pink cashmere sweater from around her neck, giving Ferdy easier access to the buttons on her shirt.

But Ferdy can't take a hint.

"Yeah," he chuckles uncertainly. "Look, we've got about fifteen minutes before the whole place locks up. We should probably head out."

Holy cow! she thinks. *Would you even touch me if I was naked, Ferdy?*

"Ferdy," Alison replies, her voice morphing from sweet to suggestive.

"Yeah?"

They smile at one another.

"Come here," Alison whispers.

Leslie stalks the first level of Park Plaza looking for her boyfriend. She's getting more infuriated with every step.

"I want my Virgin Lites!" she cries, stomping her feet like a toddler. "Mike!"

She reaches the alcove with the cigarette vending machine. A couple of the recess lights seem to have burned out, making the short hallway look deep and ominous.

"Mike?" she shouts into the darkness. "Damn you, Mike! If you don't come out right now, don't even bother."

No response.

"I know you're in there!" Leslie says. "I can smell your cheap cologne and Juicy Fruit!"

More mad than suspicious, she stomps into the alcove; she steels herself, expecting Mike to jump out like Freddy Krueger. She's ready to slap that gum right out of his mouth.

Instead, she walks right into Mike's limp body on the other side of the vending machine.

It's too dark for Leslie to see his fatal wounds or the pints of blood already drained from his body.

"All right," Leslie snaps, putting her hands on her hips. "I'm not in the mood for one of your practical jokes, Mike." She gives his thigh a little kick. "Wake up, idiot!" When her boyfriend doesn't move a muscle, her ire rises. "Wake up!" She's fed up. She leans down and shakes his shoulders. "I don't need this cra—"

Mike's skin is cold. His opened eyes are glazed over and milky. His jaw is slack and motionless. His throat is missing.

Leslie realizes she's standing in a pool of blood—Mike's blood. She's never seen so much blood in her life. The reality of the situation hits her like an avalanche.

"Mike!" Leslie screams and recoils, nearly slipping in Mike's coagulating plasma.

Without warning, the double doors leading from the service corridors burst open with a jarring crunch. Illuminated from behind, Protector 1 rushes towards Leslie like a pouncing metal panther.

"DETAIN INTRUDER!" the robot roars.

Leslie turns-tail and sprints back towards The Furniture King with Protector 1 in hot pursuit. The robot is fast, but Leslie is faster. She wasn't voted MVP of the Varsity Cross Country Team for nothing. She screams at intervals as she runs.

Protector 1 can't get close enough to grab her with its

claws. Soon, she's out of taser range and, a moment later, too far for it to land a tranquilizer dart.

GOG directs Protector 1 from above.

Activate laser beams, the supercomputer commands.

Protector 1's advanced weapons systems come online. A laser generator powers up with an ominous whine. A series of crystal lenses and artificial accelerators move into position behind the robot's visor.

"NOW DEPLOYING LASER DETERRENT," Protector 1 announces before releasing a torrent of pink beams in Leslie's direction. The lasers blast several of the mall's oversized potted plants and benches to smithereens. Still, its target is hard to get a lock on.

Leslie yelps when a laser beam nicks her right butt cheek.

The couples back at the store are all startled by the intense commotion clearly coming their way. In various states of undress, Rick and Linda, Greg and Suzie, and Ferdy and Alison run to the main showroom to see what's happening.

They can barely comprehend the scene unfolding on the other side of the glass windows.

"Oh, my..." Greg says, stunned. "Oh, my God!

"What's happening?" Suzie asks, pressing her head against her boyfriend's chest.

Similarly, Rick and Linda cling to one another in disbelief.

Ferdy and Alison stand transfixed, like statues.

"Is that..." Ferdy struggles to put what he's seeing into words. "Is that robot trying to *kill* Leslie?"

Leslie's eyes are bulging with fear as she makes a bee-line for the front doors of The Furniture King.

"Come on!" Linda screams.

"Get in here!" Rick yells to Leslie.

"What's happening?" Suzie cries.

Mere feet from the glass doors, Protector 1 finally lands a kill shot. A pink laser beam connects.

The teens in the Furniture King watch in horror as Leslie's entire head explodes off of her body. A bucket's worth of blood, pulverized brain matter, and skull fragments splatter across the front windows. If it wasn't for the glass, they'd all be drenched in the gooey remnants of their dead friend.

"Oh, my God!" Linda screams.

Suzie almost faints.

Ferdy and Alison fall into each other's arms, trembling.

Protector 1 peers down at Leslie's headless, lifeless body.

"THANK YOU," the robot says. "HAVE A NICE DAY." Protector 1 turns his attention to the targets inside The Furniture King. It signals GOG, requesting permission to initiate Annihilation Sequence Alpha Delta.

Proceed, GOG commands.

Protector 1 summons Protector 2 from the second level.

"Oh my God!" Linda screams when she sees a second robotic monstrosity coming down an escalator. "There's another one!"

CHAPTER 18

Protector 2 joins Protector 1 in front of The Furniture King.

"Protector 2, arming," the second robot announces in a voice identical to its sibling. "Assist Protector 1."

"Detain intruders," Protector 1 commands.

Side-by-side, in unison, the Protectors move in.

"Initiating Annihilation Sequence Alpha Delta," they say as one.

"They're coming right towards us!" Suzie screams.

"Quick!" Greg steps up and takes control of the situation. "Everyone, get into the storeroom. Let's go, let's go!"

Protector 1 and Protector 2 shatter the glass doors and windows with a volley of laser-fire. Protector 2's blue lasers are the only way to tell it apart from Protector 1.

The teens are showered in bits of blasted glass as they retreat.

The Protectors enter the store, firing lasers in a complex kill-pattern.

Christmas figurines are blasted to dust. Televisions and other electronics explode and smolder. Mattresses, couches, and chairs are shredded into charred pieces. It's a chaotic cacophony of retail carnage.

Suzie trips behind a couch, barely dodging a pink beam. Greg falls through a glass coffee table attempting to come to his girlfriend's rescue, nearly getting vaporized. Rick does his best to shield Linda from flying debris as they scramble.

"Go, go, go!" Greg screams, pulling Suzie by the wrist.

Alison looks momentarily stunned, uncertain what to do or where to go.

Ferdy takes her by the hand.

"Come with me if you want to live!" Ferdy yells.

They sprint into the fray. They jump on a mattress and spring across piles of burning debris. As they jump, Protector 2 turns the mattresses into ashes. They hit the ground on the other side of a smashed China cabinet and tumble into the back storeroom.

Greg, Suzie, Rick, and Linda follow Ferdy and Alison. Once everyone's inside, Greg and Rick close the storeroom's thick metal door just as a crystal chandelier crashes down in front of them. The noises outside seem to subside.

"My uncle built this room to be like Fort Knox," Ferdy says.

"This door's pretty sturdy," Rick agrees. "But I'm sure those things will be able to get inside eventually."

"Let's stack some boxes," Greg suggests. "Make a barricade."

"Let's do it," Rick concurs.

While the shirtless boys stack boxes, Suzie and Linda put the rest of their clothes back on.

"What about the fire exit?" Linda asks, pointing at the storeroom's back door,

"All that's gonna do is put us back in the line of fire of those machines," Ferdy replies.

"Beats being trapped in here," Linda, now fully dressed, protests. "Who knows what they're planning?"

"Linda's right." Rick knows better than anyone just how smart his wife is. "We've gotta get out somewhere we can run."

"It's too risky!" Ferdy insists. "I'll call 911." He scrambles over to a small desk with a phone on it and puts the receiver to his ear. The line's dead; GOG has already seen to that. But it doesn't matter, anyway.

It's midnight exactly, and the entire mall seems to rumble as giant gears turn and heavy cables engage.

"What's that noise?" Alison asks.

Greg sighs.

"That's the sound of the mall's new security system engaging," he explains. "This place is essentially inescapable until six a.m."

Throughout the mall, steel doors (each over two feet thick) roll into place over all of the Plaza's access points. They lock into place with chilling *clinks* and *clunks* that echo through the entire complex.

Suzie's heart sinks. She hates the feeling of being locked in. She struggles against an impending panic attack.

"We gotta get out of here," she whispers.

"We're gonna have to get some weapons," Rick says while finally taking a moment to put his shirt back on.

"We're never gonna get out of here!" Suzie whines, on the verge of tears.

"Yes, we are," Greg tells her as pulls his shirt on. "I promise." But even Greg's magical voice can't calm Suzie's nerves this time.

"Hey, what about that?" Alison asks, pointing at a grate on the ceiling.

Everyone else looks up.

"The air duct," Greg replies.

"That's it!" Ferdy exclaims. "We'll take it down to the parking levels and we're outta here!"

"Good plan!" Linda replies. "Let's go for it!"

"Come on, Suzie," Greg directs. "You first."

For Suzie, crawling through an HVAC duct sounds like torture, but she does her best to control her anxiety.

It sure beats getting blown up by a Go-bot, she reminds herself.

The guys hoist Suzie up to the ceiling. She gives the vent cover a few good tugs before it finally comes loose.

"Go, baby," says Greg.

On the other side of the metal door, the Protectors are making their own moves.

Protector 1 places small dabs of plasticine explosives on the door hinges with one of its utility arms. A panel on its upper left quadrant opens; hooked wires deploy from a gun barrel into the sticky blobs of C4.

What's that noise? Suzie wonders as she pulls herself into the small square air duct.

"Go, Suzie," Greg encourages, clearly failing to keep his own rising anxieties in check. "Just go!"

As soon as Suzie pulls her feet up, Rick hoists Linda.

"I'm right behind you," he promises.

"As usual," she replies, managing to joke and smile even in the face of electronic termination.

"PREPARING FOR DETONATION," Protector 1 announces.

The two robots compute their next moves.

"Proceeding to alternate access," Protector 2 announces, rolling off to initiate the next stage of their plan.

"Come on, Alison," Greg says once Linda has made it completely into the air duct. "You're next."

She's hoisted up, but pauses before following Suzie and Linda. She looks down at Ferdy.

Ferdy looks up at her and smiles as though reading her thoughts. He can't believe he met such a wonderful gal the same night as a robot uprising. *If I die tonight,* he thinks, *at least I got to kiss the girl of my dreams.*

Alison pulls herself into the air duct and calls back down.

"Come on, you guys," she says urgently. "Come on, come on!"

Before the boys can make a move, the metal door of the storeroom blasts out of its frame with incredible force. The boxes that had been stacked for extra protection are obliterated into shreds. Protector 1 rolls in, pinks lasers blazing.

There's no time for anyone else to shimmy into the air duct. Greg, Rick, and Ferdy are forced to flee out the back door and into the unknown.

CHAPTER 19

"What's happening?" Suzie screams from inside the air duct when she hears the explosion below. "Greg!"

"He's okay," Alison assures her. "They all ran out the fire exit."

"Oh, thank God!" Linda says.

"But we can't do back down," Alison continues. "One of those tin-cans is still down there and there's no telling where the other one is."

"What are we gonna do?" Suzie asks, tears flowing.

"Let's stick to Ferdy's plan," Alison replies. "If we can get to the parking levels, we can get out and call for help."

"Good idea," Linda agrees.

Alison takes the lead, crawling on her hands and knees; Linda follows close behind.

"Oh, God..." Suzie cries before reluctantly taking up the rear.

What Alison and Linda don't know is that Suzie is extremely claustrophobic.

At age seven, while playing hide and seek with her cousins in Oklahoma, Suzie was accidentally locked in an abandoned refrigerator behind a dilapidated slaughterhouse. For over an hour, no one could find her, and no one could hear her screaming. The oppressive darkness and rancid odors were made worse by a mid-summer heatwave. Suzie was half-cooked and unconscious when her aunts and uncles finally found her.

Though traumatized, Suzie realizes that her early brush with death inspired her to make the most of life. She never bothers with gossip or unnecessary drama because, who needs it? For Suzie, every day is Friday and every night is Prom Night.

Being locked in the mall awakened her old anxieties. Being cornered in the storeroom made her imagine being back in that sweltering refrigerator. Being forced into the air duct, however, undid over a decade of therapy. Her resolve crumbles as her mind summersaults close to madness.

"Is it getting hot in here?" Suzie asks, barely able to contain her panic.

"Yeah," Linda replies. "I thought this was an air conditioning duct?"

"HVAC stands for heating, ventilation, *and* air-conditioning," Alison explains. "It's all the same thing."

"So, why is the heat turned up—in the middle of summer?" Linda wonders.

"Well," Alison says, thinking, "these robots and doors must be run by a central computer, and that computer must have access to the mall's systems."

"Which mean-" Linda says.

"They know we're here!" Suzie interrupts. "They're trying to French-Fry us."

"Come on, Suze," Alison says. "You-know-who gives you twice as much heat at the restaurant!"

The air ducts are suddenly entirely too hot. Blisters are in danger of forming on the palms of their hands.

"Damn!" Linda winces. "This really burns."

"Wrap whatever you can around your hands," Alison suggests, pulling the sleeves of her cashmere sweater over her hands.

"I can't stand this anymore!" Suzie says. "I gotta get outta here. I gotta get outta here!"

"Come on, Suze," Alison says. "Hang in there."

"NO!" Suzie is going off the deep-end. "I gotta find Greg. He needs me. Let me outta here!"

"Suzie, please," Alison says. "The guys told us to go down to the parking levels."

"Come on, kiddo," Linda says. "Greg wouldn't want you to give up now."

An irrational, angry side of Suzie bubbles to the surface.

"Oh, go to Hell, Linda!" Suzie's outburst shocks her friends, who've never seen this side of her before. "You do what you want!" she yells, on the verge of hyperventilating. "But I'm getting out of here!"

Alison tries to use the same voice her father uses when he's being strict with her.

"Suzie, stop it!" she says. "Pull yourself together."

Old traumas and new horrors reach a boiling point. Suzie is simply not herself.

"Greg needs me!" she says, her voice shrill. "I know he does!" She breaks away from Alison and Linda, turning back towards another vent cover they passed a few yards back.

"Come back!" Linda cries in vain.

"We've got to go back for her!" Alison says.

"I really don't think that's a good idea," Linda says.

"I know," Alison says, "But the way things are heating up in here, we might not make it to the parking levels anyway. It's getting hotter than Luigi's oven!"

"Alright," Linda says. "Let's go after her."

Before Linda and Alison can catch up to her, Suzie has already kicked out another vent cover. She's so overwhelmed by the sensations of being crushed and cooked, she doesn't even look down before jumping from the simmering air duct.

"I wonder what store this is?" Linda says.

"There's only one way to find out," Alison says.

Hoping for the best, Linda and Alison hop out of the air duct, and into the unknown.

The trio gets up off the floor, covered in dust and cobwebs. They brush themselves off and look around, finding themselves inside the mall's hardware store, A Bucket of Bolts. Everything suggests they're safe—for the moment.

"Let's go find Greg!" Suzie shouts. Escaping the air duct has her feeling reinvigorated—like She-Ra, Princess of Power.

"Really," Linda replies. "That's not a good idea. If we can get to the parking levels, we have a better chance at calling for help."

"Bullshit!" Suzie the Warrior Princess replies. "Greg could be hurt. They all could. I'm gonna find them. I've got to!"

Alison turns to Linda.

"What do you think?"

"I think trying to get to the parking levels is safer," Linda replies. "But we can't let Suzie go off alone. We don't roll like that."

Alison nods.

"Agreed!" she replies. "Don't run off yet, Suzie. We're going with you!

"And, if we gotta go," Linda adds, looking over at a shelf stocked with gallon-cans of gas, "let's not go empty handed."

CHAPTER 20

Back when they were kids, Ferdy, Greg, Rick, and Mike used to run around parks and playgrounds pretending to be Rambo or G.I. Joe, Indiana Jones or Capitan Kirk. They'd won pretend battles against communists and terrorists, Nazis and even extraterrestrials. And while they could never have imagined facing off against angry androids in real life, their childhood games have oddly prepared them for a moment like this.

After narrowly escaping the wrath of Protector 1 in the storeroom, the boys come bursting out of the service corridors and back onto the first level of the Plaza. Greg's shoulder still smarts from his brush with laser shrapnel. With no Protectors in sight, they huddle up to make a gameplan.

"What now?" Ferdy asks Greg and Rick.

"Find some way outta here," Greg suggests. "If we can find another air duct, maybe we can meet the girls on the parking levels."

"And what if the girls can't make it to the parking lot and come back?" Rick asks before answering his own question. "No. We're gonna have to defend ourselves. This is like *Red*

Dawn and this mall is like America. If we're gonna take our country back, we need guns!"

Greg and Ferdy know just the place.

"Peckinpah's!" they say in unison.

"Let's go," Rick says.

Peckinpah's Sporting Goods is also on the first level of Park Plaza just a few dozen yards away. Greg, Rick, and Ferdy make certain the coast is clear before running silently in combat formation. It isn't long before they're standing at the shop's front door.

"How are we gonna get in?" Ferdy asks.

"Don't worry," Rick says, reaching into an oversized potted plant and retrieving a fist-sized stone. "I got the keys." Rick throws the rock like a major league pitcher pitching a no-hitter.

Peckinpah's front window shatters and rains down in a shimmering cascade.

"Jesus!" Ferdy's impressed.

So is Greg.

Darting into the store, Rick channels Patrick Swayze and starts calling the shots.

"Ferdy, propane tanks!" he orders. "Grab the biggest one you can find."

"Yes, Sir!" Ferdy replies, springing into action.

"Greg," Rick continues. "Come with me to the gun aisle."

Like every mall sporting goods store in the 1980s, Peckinpah's has a wide variety of firearms available for immediate purchase. Everything from shotguns to Uzis, from handguns to sniper rifles.

None of the boys have any military training, of course. East Beverly High doesn't even have an ROTC. But Rick and Greg recently watched *Commando* together and are confident they know what they're doing.

Rick grabs himself an AR and a sniper rifle for back-up.

"Grab yourself a shotgun, Greg."

"Good idea," Greg replies. "What caliber shells do I use?"

"Twelve gauge," Rick tells him. "On the shelf over there."

"Got it," Greg replies.

"Grab me some 223s while you're over there."

"Sure thing."

"Thanks."

Ferdy, lugging an eight gallon propane tank, finds his friends in the gun aisle.

"Arm yourself, Ferdy," Rick tells him.

"All right!" Ferdy knows exactly what he wants: a Smith & Wesson .44 Magnum.

"Everyone locked and loaded?" Greg asks.

"Yes, Sir," Greg and Ferdy reply.

Rick smiles.

"Let's go send those mechanical fuckers a Rambo-Gram!"

Feeling empowered and invincible, Greg, Rick and Ferdy head to the center of Level One, itching to kill some androids.

Greg leads the way like an ace tracker clearing a path through the jungle. Behind him, Greg's shotgun is pumped and chambered; he's wearing a bandoleer packed with additional ammunition. Ferdy's got a propane tank in his left hand, and a gun that can stop a train in his right hand.

Greg looks over at Ferdy. The humongous gun looks out of place in his friend's hand. He chuckles.

"You sure you know how to shoot that?" he chides.

"Yeah," Ferdy replies confidently. "I saw *Dirty Harry* twenty-four times!" He holds up the barrel of his .44 and flashes Greg his most menacing mug.

"Let's make their day!" Greg says.

They halt near the center of Park Plaza's expansive open courtyard. From there, they can just about see every shop on every level. The protectors are nowhere to be seen.

"I think it's time to make our presence known," Rick announces. "Are you guys all set?"

"Yeah," Ferdy replies, gritting his teeth with determination and anticipation.

"Ready," Greg says in a calm voice that conveys focus and resolve.

"Good," Rick says. "Let's get this party started."

He fires his assault rifle into the air, shattering several panes of glass in the Plaza's expansive skylight in the process. The booming cracks echo throughout the mall as bits of glass rain down. Smoke wafts from Rick's rifle barrel.

Greg states the obvious: "One of them ought to have heard that."

"A dead man could've heard that!" Ferdy says.

As though on cue, Protector 1 comes barreling towards them, full steam, from the south wing of the Plaza.

"Hey, fellas," Ferdy says. "We got company."

"That didn't take very long," Greg says.

Everyone points their weapon at the robot careening towards them.

"Steady..." Rick says, waiting until everyone's got a clear shot.

"Detain intruders," Protector 1 says.

"Go for it!" Rick yells.

The trio start unloading their guns on Protector 1—but nothing can penetrate its chrome titanium shell. Their bullets bounce and crack into hot scraps of shrapnel—and now, the robot's almost on top of them.

"Take cover!" Rick shouts.

Greg finds a new position a few yards away behind a stairwell. Rick and Ferdy find cover behind one of the Plaza's ridiculously oversized potted plants.

"ENGAGING LASER DETERRENT," Protector 1 says in its bowel-quaking voice before initiating a relentless stream of pink lasers.

"Ferdy!" Rick yells above the bullets and laser blasts. "Throw the tank now!"

Ferdy grabs the propane tank with both hands and flings it over his head at the robot, like Donkey Kong throwing a barrel at Mario. It's a perfect throw, landing a few feet in front of Protector 1 before sliding and lodging into its front treads.

"Go for it, Rick!" Greg yells, still furiously pumping his shotgun.

Rick switches to the sniper rifle, aims at the propane tank, and fires.

BOOM.

A massive ball of burning gas blasts Protector 1 off of its base, leaving it upturned and powerless like a dead turtle. Its inner circuitry sizzles and pops as smoke bellows from its cooling vents. A bubbling, viscous fluid flows from its dented body.

Rick, Greg, and Ferdy investigate cautiously.

"Jesus." Ferdy's practically nauseated by the stench of the gunk pooling around Protector 1. "What's that?"

"Robot blood," Rick says.

"Good job, fellas!" Ferdy rejoices. "Not too shabby, huh?" He's proud of his gunslinging prowess.

"We're not finished yet," Greg says. "We still got two more of these suckers around here someplace."

"We gotta get more tanks," Rick tells his friends, "And I've got an idea."

CHAPTER 21

Inside A Bucket of Bolts Hardware, Linda is explaining to Suzie and Alison the basics on how to make bombs out of rags and gas cans.

"Right," she says, demonstrating. "Take the cap off and stuff the cloth in."

"That's it?" Alison asks.

"That's it," Linda replies. "Light it and throw it."

"You sound like you've done this before," Alison says.

"Regular or unleaded," Linda says, smiling. "It gets the job done."

As Linda and Suzie make bombs, Alison spots a box of flares on display.

Why get caught in a dangerous situation? the product sign asks. *Protect your family for $2.99!*

Family. The word makes Alison think of her father. She regrets lying to him about the party now more than ever. She knows he'll be devastated if anything happens to his only daughter, and the thought of it devastates Alison.

"If any boy tries to get in your shirt or your pants," he would often say, "light up a flare and I'll come running!"

Alison wishes her father could swoop in and rescue her now, rescue all of them from this techno-nightmare. She grabs a flare; holding it in her hand makes her feel better, somehow—more secure. It's too big to fit in her pocket so Alison stuffs it in her shirt.

Ironic, she thinks. *Daddy might get a kick out of this.*

As the young ladies continue making bombs, the sound of distant gunfire echoes through the mall. The ladies stop what they're doing and listen. A moment later, a loud *boom* causes all the windows around them to rattle. And then—silence.

"Do you think that was the boys?" Suzie asks.

"It must have been," Linda says.

"Do you think they got one?" Alison asks.

"It sure sounds like it," Linda replies.

"Let's go!" Suzie says. "They need our help!"

In another part of the mall, a debilitated, barely functional Protector 1 receives signals from GOG. The supercomputer works quickly to repair its minion, rebuilding internal systems and replacing corrupted data. The robot is, essentially, healing.

It takes two of Protector 1's powerful arms pushing against the ground for the machine to right itself. Once back on its wheels, it runs a preliminary systems check. It tests its motors and points of articulation; it realigns its processors and refocuses its visor. Its weapons systems power back up.

"PROTECTOR 1 BACK ONLINE."

CHAPTER 22

The boys reconvene with half a dozen propane tanks on the second level, where the Plaza's famous glass elevator is parked. It's time to initiate the next phase of the plan.

Ferdy presses the button for the elevator, but the doors won't open.

"It's not working," he reports.

"Shit," Greg says. "I was afraid of that."

"Never hurts to try," Ferdy says.

"Move aside, Ferdy," Rick says. "Give me a hand. Let's pry this baby open."

Together, they do their best to pry and pull the elevator doors open.

"Come on," Rick grunts.

"Keep pulling," Greg says.

"You know," Ferdy says. "I've got a worry."

"Report from the front," Greg says. "Ferdy's got a worry."

"I was just wondering if these robots can read our minds," says Ferdy.

"Well," Rick replies. "They're gonna be awful mad when they get to me."

The doors to the glass elevator finally give, allowing the boys to get inside.

"All right!" Rick finds the rescue hatch on the ceiling of the elevator and pulls it open. A moment later, he's shimmying out and on top of the car. "You're next, Greg."

Once up top with Rick, Greg calls down to Ferdy.

"Pass us up three or four of those propane tanks, Ferdy."

"10-4." After passing the tanks up to Greg and Rick, he turns his attention to the elevator call buttons just outside the doors. This is Ferdy's time to shine. He was pissed off when his parents sent him to Engineering Camp in 9th Grade, but he's happy to have that seemingly useless knowledge now.

Ferdy uses a screwdriver to open up the call button panel. Next, he identifies the signal inputs and reverses their connections. A few more adjustments, and they should be all set.

Simultaneously, Greg and Rick are fixing propane tanks around the elevator's motor, pulleys, and cables. The idea is to catch one of the robots inside in order to blow it to Kingdom Come. Someone will have to shoot the propane tank from a downward trajectory, but when one tank blows, all the others will pop off with it.

"Hey, guys," Ferdy calls up while fiddling with some wires. "How's it goin'?"

"We're almost done, Ferdy," Greg replies. "Hey," he says to Rick. "You think Mike got out all right?"

"Aw, shit," Rick replies. "Mike… For his sake, I hope so. Right now, I'm more concerned about the girls."

"You and me both," Greg says. "Are you sure this is gonna work?"

"I can't lie," Rick replies ominously. "With those things, Greg, I'm not sure of anything."

"Ferdy!" Greg calls down through the escape hatch. "How's the panel coming?"

"The doors work," he's clearly thrilled to report. "I bypassed the circuit. But going up or down is controlled by the mall's computer. We'll just have to see where it goes."

"Shouldn't be an issue," Ricks says. "As long as we're all in position."

Greg stands up and scans the mall in all directions. Everything's quiet—unnervingly so.

"Do you hear anything unusual?" Greg asks.

"Only my heartbeat," says Ferdy.

CHAPTER 23

Close by, Suzie, Linda, and Alison are finishing their sweep of the first level, proceeding cautiously. Their gas bombs are ready to deploy. Tensions are running high.

"It's so quiet," Alison says.

"Yeah." Linda agrees. "Too quiet."

Protector 2 is no longer docked in its communications alcove. Its new directives have it on an intercept course. Its treads are so stealthy, it's almost upon them before anyone notices.

"DETAIN INTRUDERS," Protector 2 blares, releasing bursts of blue lasers.

Suzie screams incessantly; practically petrified with fear. Alison and Linda drag her to safety behind another oversized potted plant.

"Set it off, Alison!" Linda yells.

Alison sets one of the gasoline bombs on the floor, lights the cloth with a cigarette lighter, and pushes it across the floor towards Protector 2 with the precision of an Olympic curler. It comes to a stop directly in front of the robot before exploding like a meteorite, erupting into flames.

It's enough to stop Protector 2 in its tracks—but only momentarily. All the Protectors are fireproof and heat-resistant up to ten-thousand degrees. The explosion and resulting fire barely register as a blip in its data log. It continues unfazed through the gushing flames.

"No!" Suzie cries. "It's not stopping!"

"Come on!" Linda hollers at Alison and Suzie. "Let's head towards the courtyard."

The girls make a break for it, but Protector 2 zaps Suzie above her right hell, immediately severing her Achilles' tendon. She falls to the ground with her unused gas bombs, gripped by unimaginable pain and new echelons of panic. Her screams become blood cuddling.

As Linda and Alison take cover behind another oversized potted plant, Rick, Greg, and Ferdy round a corner just in time to see Protector 2 bearing down on Suzie.

"Help me!" Suzie's cries are beyond desperate. "Help me up!"

"We've gotta help her!" Linda screams.

"Suzie, I'm coming!" Greg yells, readying his shotgun.

"THANK YOU," Protector 2 declares. "HAVE A NICE DAY." It fires a couple of laser pulses at Suzie's gas bombs, setting them both off with another window-rattling explosion.

Suzie goes up in flames, screaming in anguish.

Suzie hasn't been blown to bits. It would have been better if she had. Instead, she's burning to a crisp—alive. The sounds of it, the smells of it, the sight of it all is more than anyone can fathom.

"Suzie!" Greg screams, running into the fray.

Suzie's screams reach an unnatural pitch—like a whistle. She's trying to stand up, but she can't. Worst of all, there's nothing anyone can do to help her.

Suzie makes one last flailing attempt to stand. Her skin's

charred and sloughing off; boiling blood comes bubbling out of her mouth and nostrils. The Aqua-Net in her hair makes her head burn like a Roman candle.

Finally—thankfully—Suzie slumps down for the last time. Her body crumbles, like a campfire falling in on itself. Her voice is gone. Only the popping and crackling of the blaze remains.

And the smell.

No one's more shocked and devastated than Greg. He's watching the love of his life disintegrating into ash. But there's no time to mourn.

Rick snaps him out of his trance.

"Come on!" he yells, shaking Greg's shoulder. "We've got to trap that motherfucker in the elevator, remember?"

"You fucking bastard!" Greg screams before lobbing shots at Protector 2.

"Ferdy!" Rick yells. "Get Linda and Alison someplace safe!"

Greg's rage is only rising. He fires nonstop at Protector 2 until it finally acknowledges him.

"Detain intruder," it says.

Rick has to pull Greg away.

"Forget it, Greg! Bullets don't work!"

Greg ignores him, seemingly intent on making his last stand.

"Suzie wouldn't want you to die for her, man!" Rick pleads. "Suzie would want you to help protect the others!"

"You're right, Rick," he says finally. "Let's catch up with the others."

CHAPTER 24

Rick and Greg run after Linda, Alison, and Ferdy, occasionally firing their guns behind them as they go. They reconnect with their friends as Ferdy leads them up an escalator.

Soon, they reach the second level.

"Keep going!" Rick shouts at Ferdy. "Take everyone to Level Three! I'll get that thing into the elevator."

Ferdy leads Alison and Linda up the next escalator.

"Be careful!" Linda calls down to Rick as the escalator continues to separate them.

"I love you."

"Let me help you, Rick," Greg says.

"No," Rick replies, handing him his sniper rifle. "Take it. Suzie would want you to protect the others. Besides, I'm going to need all of you shooting at those tanks if we're going to pull this off."

Greg nods. He turns and follows the others up to Level Three.

Protector 2 makes its way towards the escalator on the second level, firing its blue beams as soon as it has a line of sight.

Greg runs up the escalator after the others, shotgun in his right hand, sniper rifle in the left.

Rick waves his arms in order to get Protector 2's full attention.

"Look at me!" he hollers before tossing his AR over the ledge and down to the first floor. "I'm unarmed! Come and get me!"

Protector 2 doesn't have to be asked twice.

"Detain intruder," it growls, speeding after the target. The robot sees Rick getting into the glass elevator. "Detain intruder!"

Rick smiles and waves as the elevator doors close between them.

Rick is gone. Protector 2 proceeds inside the elevator to confirm its target's escape, automatically flipping Ferdy's trip-switch. The doors close behind it. Protector 2 is trapped.

Rick pulls himself onto the roof of the elevator through the escape hatch in the nick of time. As he makes some final adjustments to the propane tanks, the others line up against a railing across from him on Level Three, forty yards away.

Greg hands his shotgun off to Linda. Everyone gets into position and stands firm, aiming their weapons at the propane tanks on top of the elevator; all except for Alison, who doesn't have a gun. Everyone's focused and ready for Rick's signal.

Rick turns the knob on a loose propane tank, releasing a hissing stream of flammable gas. He opens the trap door and looks down at the confused robot, turning in circles.

"Hey, Oscar the Grouch," he calls down to it. "I've got a present for you!" With that, he drops the hissing tank into the elevator before slamming the hatch closed again.

"Now!" Rick calls out to his friends. He quickly leaps from the roof of the elevator and tumbles out of sight.

"Everyone fire!" Greg yells—and they do.

Linda, Ferdy, and Greg fire on the propane tanks, but forty yards is no easy target. Their ammunition is beginning to dwindle and Linda and Greg are getting noticeably frustrated.

Alison, however, has had enough of standing idly by.

"Give me your gun, Ferdy!" She doesn't even ask permission before yanking it out of his hand. She spreads her feet for better footing before aligning the site at the tip of the .44 with the cluster of propane tanks on top of the elevator.

Alison takes her shot—she only needs one.

It's the biggest explosion any of them have seen or felt. The entire Plaza rattles on its foundations.

The lift cables snap, sending the glass elevator plummeting down to Sublevel Four. The impact sets off another series of explosions that gush up the elevator shaft like a volcano blowing lava. It's almost overpowering, close to deafening, and practically blinding.

Everyone stands there in amazement—especially Ferdy.

"Nice shot!" he tells Alison when his senses return. "How'd you get so good?"

Alison shrugs.

"Dad's a Marine," she replies nonchalantly.

Once the smoke clears, Linda scans the lower levels for any sign of Rick.

As though on cue, Rick emerges from the smoke and dust, smiling up at her.

CHAPTER 25

It was Alison's idea to hide out back at Uncle Luigi's Pizzeria & Restaurante. She has a key and they still have time to kill before the impenetrable security doors open at 6 a.m. Laying low seems like the best option.

Ferdy's on lookout. He's crouched down by the door, looking for any signs of robot activity. Alison sits beside him, in need of company. Rick and Linda are sitting at a table against the wall, lost in their own thoughts—trying to make sense of it all.

Greg's sitting alone against the bar. He's helped himself to a few beers—and he's not looking so hot.

"How many of them do you think are left?" Alison asks Ferdy.

"At least one," Ferdy says. "There's one for each level. We killed the first one before we found you guys, and that was number two in the elevator. I guess we haven't seen number three yet."

"Hopefully we never will," Alison replies.

"According to my calculations," Linda says to Rick, "and

provided we survive the night, of course, we're gonna be in hock to this place for the next eighty-five years."

Rick slaps a fresh magazine into his AR.

"How many tune-ups is that, Linda?" he asks.

"Just a sec." She begins a new calculation, factoring in a couple of postulations and updating appropriate ratios. "Two-million-nine-hundred-thousand-four-hundred-thirty-one."

Rick considers the implications for a moment.

"Maybe we should raise our rates." Rick and his wife smile at one another, offering small comforts. Rick turns his attention to Alison. "Hey, dead-eye."

"Yo," Alison says.

"Nice shootin'," Rick replies with a thankful smile.

"Thanks."

"Tell me one thing, though, huh?" It's Greg. This is the first time Greg has spoken in over an hour, and he's drunk as a skunk. He can still smell Suzie's burning flesh in his nostrils. He doubts he'll ever be able to eat barbecue again. "Why did you leave the air shaft?" he asks, drilling his eyes into Alison. "I mean, you were safe there. You were safe!"

"It's not Alison's fault," Linda tells Greg.

"Suzie thought you were in trouble," Alison says. "She just wanted to help."

"I'm telling you," Greg says through clenched teeth. "You should've kept her there!"

Ferdy comes to Alison's defense.

"She told you what happened," he snaps. "Why don't you just leave her alone?" Ferdy almost never stands up to his friends; it's a rare act of defiance.

"Shut up!" Greg yells. "You just shut the fuck up!" It's the first time anyone's seen him truly angry—and it scares them.

"Hey!" Rick snaps at Greg. "Do you mind keeping it

down? There's another one of those things out there, and you're gonna bring it right to us!"

Everyone goes quiet for a moment, but Alison has a nagging question.

"Why haven't we seen the third one yet?" she asks.

"Why?" Greg says, slightly slurring his words. "I'll tell you why. It's because the fucker's out there waiting for us!" Greg slaps his leg, becoming even more animated. "That robot's waiting to pick us off one by one! But I got news for you. He ain't getting me!" Greg begins reloading his shotgun. "I'm going after that fucker myself!"

"Greg, you're not thinking, man," Rick says in his most calming voice. "We got this far by staying together."

"And a lot of good that did Suzie, right?" Greg's face is turning red. The tendons in his neck are bulging and he's starting to sweat.

"Wait!" Ferdy says, sitting up. "I've got an idea. I remember hearing that the robots are controlled by a master computer in a control room somewhere on the third level. We shut it down, it shuts the robots down!"

"It's worth a try," Rick replies reluctantly.

"Computer, huh?" Greg says before getting to his feet. "Let's go trash the fucker!"

CHAPTER 26

Greg bolts out of Uncle Luigi's Pizzeria & Restaurante like a marine storming the beach at Normandy.

"Come on, guys!" he hollers. "Let's take out that master computer!"

"Wait!" Ferdy calls after him as he and the others follow. "Slow down!"

Greg isn't listening. He runs up an escalator to the second level.

"Greg, will you wait!" Linda yells. "This wasn't part of the plan!"

"Man!" Ferdy says. "He's losin' it!"

"We'll be lucky if he doesn't get us all killed," Alison says.

"Greg, stop!" yells Linda.

"Greg, wait!" pleads Rick.

"Greg!" Ferdy is beside himself. "Please! Stop!"

Greg isn't listening. He's like a man possessed. He's got vengeance to dispense. Without pausing, he hops another escalator to the third floor. He turns around as the conveyance continues taking him up.

"Come on, guys!" he calls down to the second level. "The coast is clear!"

The coast isn't clear.

Protector 3 emerges from the darkness, just as Greg reaches the top of the escalator. Before he can turn around, the titanium beast grabs Greg by the back of his neck and lifts him off the ground in one of its powerful claws.

Greg's spinal column cracks open at the base of his neck. He screams as the rest of his body falls limp, paralyzed.

Protector 3's arm extends. With a quick motion, it tosses Greg's entire body over the escalator railing.

Greg screams as he falls through the open-air center of the mall, down to the hard polished tiles floors on Level One. He lands with a thud and a splash. His head pops like a melon.

It happens so fast, no one has time to respond until it's over.

"Greg," Linda screams. "Greg, no!"

"Greg!" Ferdy groans.

"THANK YOU," Protector 3 says. "HAVE A NICE DAY."

And then there were four.

From the second level, Rick, Linda, and Ferdy open fire on Protector 3. Just like the other Protectors, though, the robot is impervious to bullets.

Protector 3 maneuvers onto the down escalator, setting its sights on the remaining survivors.

"DETAIN INTRUDERS," it says.

"We can't stop it!" Ferdy says.

"Fall back and regroup!" Rick commands.

The quartet find a staircase around the corner and race down. As they're approaching Level One, however, they're greeted with a most unwelcome sight: Protector 1 is now moving in to intercept the group at the bottom.

"No way!" Ferdy yells, stopping in his tracks.

"It's the first one!" Alison screams. "You didn't kill it."

As the group stands stunned, Protector 3 reaches the second level and begins closing in from above.

"Protector 3 to Level Two," it announces. "Detain intruders."

"Detain intruders," Protector 1 reiterates.

"I've got an idea!" Ferdy yells. "We've got to get into one of the department stores."

"O'Dell's is right around the corner," Linda replies.

"Let's go!" Rick says, leading the way.

O'Dell's was one of the four massive department stores anchoring the four corners of Park Plaza. Whereas most shops in the mall have glass doors and minimal security, department stores are protected at night by rolling metal covers, like garage doors.

They reach the closed entrance to O'Dell's on Level Two.

Ferdy slides to the floor, attempting to pop the heavy lock holding the shutter in place. It's no use.

"Step aside," Rick says to Ferdy. "I've got the key." He aims his AR at the lock, and fires. The mechanism shatters, but the door won't budge.

"It's still stuck!" Ferdy yells.

"Let's get it unstuck," Rick urges. "And fast!"

Protector 1 and Protector 3 have regrouped on the second level. They speed towards the teenagers in unison, deterrent systems at full power.

"Detain intruders," they say as one.

"Come on!" Linda screams.

"There's no time!" Alison says. "We're not gonna make it!"

Ferdy jams the barrel of his .44 under the gate and pops the locking mechanism. The door rolls upward—but only a few inches. "I hope everyone's feeling skinny," he says. "Help me hold this up, Rick. Come on!"

Rick manages to get the metal door up a few more inches. "Go," he yells at Linda.

Linda lies flat on her back and squeezes into O'Dell's.

"Alison," Ferdy says. "You're next."

Alison follows Linda under the gap as Protectors 1 and 3 come around a corner, straight towards them.

"DETAIN INTRUDERS."

Protector 1 shoots short bursts of pink lasers. Protector 3 follows suit, delivering a volley of green blasts. One of them nicks Alison on her right arm as she shimmies into O'Dell's.

Alison yelps and grimaces.

"Alison!" Ferdy yells as he follows her into O'Dell's by sliding on his belly. "Alison, are you alright?"

"I think so," she replies, applying pressure to her flesh wound.

Rick grunts and pants as he pulls himself under the rolling metal doors.

Once all four of them are inside, Ferdy slams the gate down—seconds before the robots arrive.

"Where to, now?" Rick asks.

"If we're still going to find the master computer," Ferdy replies, "we need to go to the third floor. The escalator is this way." He points into the dark department store.

"What about the doors?" Alison asks. "If the lock's broken, won't the robots be able to get inside?"

"Maybe so," Rick replies. "Maybe not." He looks around and finds a twisted scrap of metal debris by his foot. He jams it into the pulley mechanism. "That should at least make things harder for them."

"Let's go!" Alison says as the four friends dart deeper inside O'Dell's.

On the other side of the metal gate, Protector 1 and Protector 3 reassess their strategy.

GOG signals Protector 3: *Attempt entry at Level Three.*

"AFFIRMATIVE," Protector 3 replies, as it rolls away.

GOG signals Protector 1: *Activate laser saw.*

"AFFIRMATIVE," Protector 1 replies. It focuses an intense beam of pink laser light at the metal door and begins cutting through it. Sparks fly as blue smoke wafts into the air.

"What's that noise?" Alison asks.

"I don't know," Linda responds, "And I don't *want* to know."

"This way!" Ferdy leads everyone towards the escalator. "Up here!"

They run to the next level.

"The exit's this way." Ferdy points.

"Hold it, Ferdy." Rick grabs him by the shoulder. Everyone pauses beside a glass counter in the makeup and perfume department. "One of them might be out there waiting for us."

"Yeah," Linda says. "We're safer in here—at least for the moment."

CHAPTER 27

Jamal Jerome pokes his shaggy head out from his dark lair in the service corridors on Level Three. He looks up and down the hallway vigilantly, squinting; his nostrils twitch. The coast appears to be clear, so he squeezes his shaggy body out of his alcove.

He knows that the mall will be opening in a couple hours—and he's hungry.

Jamal used to work at Tape World on the third floor of Park Plaza.

He's made many poor decisions over the course of his lifetime. Like when he stole four kilos of marijuana from the Mexican Cartel and tried to hide it in his work locker. The crop was so dank, the entire third level of Park Plaza smelled like Reggae Sunsplash.

When the source of the skunky odor was discovered, Jamal was immediately fired without prejudice. He packed his work locker and left out of the backdoor, head hung low. He wondered if his life could get any worse.

He'd thought about his predicament as he walked through the service corridors toward the freight elevator. If he didn't have a job, he wouldn't be able to pay rent. If he couldn't pay rent, he wouldn't have a place to live. If he didn't have a place to live, he'd be homeless.

Plus, the Mexican cartel wanted to kill him.

It was quite the pickle.

Jamal had emerged from his thoughts and realized he had no idea where he was. The service corridors were like a catacomb, and it was easy to get turned around if you weren't careful. Jamal had kept his cool for a while, but after wandering for hours, he began to wonder if he'd fallen into an alternate dimension—a liminal realm of hallways and backrooms.

Eventually, he'd found himself standing before a strange gap between walls; a dark space barely big enough to squeeze through. Within, Jamal found an area the size of a studio apartment that had somehow been walled off unintentionally. It looked like a good enough place for him to smoke some weed and get his bearings.

That was three years ago, and Jamal has been living there ever since. He sleeps all day, every day. But at night, he emerges.

Jamal's body isn't actually hairy. He wears a long fur coat that he stole from Emerson's Department Store. It's the most comfortable thing he's ever worn and he hardly ever takes it off. He roams the Plaza barefoot so as not to make any sounds, occasionally dodging security guards.

He's been cut off from the world for years, and knows nothing about the legend of Mall Mole, nor of the fact that its *his* presence at Park Plaza-the fur coat and long shaggy hair, the late night clandestine excursions, the inexplicably pilfered goods-is the inspiration for *all* of the mall's cryptozoological rumors.

Jamal emerges from the service corridors on Level Three

and makes his way towards the food court. He's trying to decide what he's in the mood; stir-fry, pizza, hamburgers-

"May I see your identification badge, please."

The terrifying voice nearly gives Jamal a heart attack.

"Yo, dude!" His voice has a distinctively Southern-Californian drawl. "It's not cool to sneak up on people like that, man…"

"May I see your identification badge," Protector 3 repeats.

"Am I high?"

"May I see your identification badge. Final request."

Jamal doesn't know if he should laugh or run away.

"Uh… how about I just go back the way I came and you-"

"Arming laser deterrent," Protector 3 announces. "Detain intruder."

"Hey little guy, no need for-"

Protector 3 fires a green laser burst towards Jamal. It narrowly misses, shattering the windows of a nearby store.

"Holy crap!" Jamal turns around and runs as fast as he can. He feels laser beams whipping past him over his shoulders. "Leave me alone!" he screams.

"Detain intruder."

Jamal crashes back into the third-floor service corridors with Protector 3 on his heels. He hopes he can give the robot the slip in the labyrinthine hallways.

"Detain anti-consumer." Protector 3 fires at Jamal unremittingly while closing the distance between them.

A few more twists and turns and Jamal can see the gap to his alcove.

No way that thing'll be able to follow me in there, he thinks.

Mere feet from safety, Protector 3 fires a tranquilizer dart at Jamal. It hits the squatter on the left heel of his bare foot.

"Whoa!" Jamal is overcome by waves of numbness; he can taste copper in the back of his throat. His vision goes blurry.

With all of his strength, he leaps towards his hidden lair as Protector 3 unleashes a fresh stream of lasers.

Beams hit the walls with pulverizing force, causing them to crack, and cave in on themselves. When the smoke and dust clears, Protector 3 sees no trace of the anti-consumer. The gap between the walls is sealed with debris.

"Thank you. Have a nice day."

CHAPTER 28

Uncertain how to proceed, the terrified teenagers regroup at O'Dell's. As time slips by, their adrenaline levels drop and exhaustion creeps in.

Rick and Linda are asleep. She's resting her head on his chest.

Ferdy's sitting with his legs pulled up to his chest and his head down. He's not asleep but he isn't actually awake either, intermittently nodding off and then waking with a start, again and again.

Alison, however, is wide awake. She moves over next to Ferdy and puts her head on his shoulder.

Ferdy stirs. He sees Alison smiling at him and smiles back before putting his arm around her. They find comfort in one another.

They're all running out of time.

On the second level, Protector 1 has completed cutting out a section of the security gate protecting O'Dell's. The cut portion falls to the floor with an echoing *slam*.

Linda and Rick are instantly startled awake.

"It's in!" Linda says.

"Yeah," Alison replies, "and it won't be long before it comes our way."

Everyone climbs to their feet.

"We've gotta get outta here," Ferdy says. "Come on!"

"Not so fast," says Rick. "One of them could've doubled back. We could get picked off out there."

"If those things want some target practice," Alison says, "then why don't we give 'em some targets?"

Rick, Linda, and Ferdy have no idea what Alison has in mind, until they follow her eye-line, and see that she's eyeing some nearby mannequins.

CHAPTER 29

The rolling metal door protecting O'Dell's Department Store's third floor entrance slowly opens.

Alerted by the noise, Protector 3 moves into position. It raises its arms menacingly and prepares to activate a variety of deterrents. When the door is fully opened, Protector 3 registers eleven targets. There's a man wearing a dress shirt with slacks and a bride. There's a woman in lingerie and another wearing sporty shorts. Someone is wearing blue pajamas, and another has a maroon sweater...

"Recalibrating trajectory," Protector 3 announces. "Initiating kill pattern Beta Epsilon. Detain intruders." The robot powers up its lasers and raises all four of its arms, claws snapping manically.

Protector 3 moves in on the mannequins.

"Ferdy!" Rick yells from his position among the decoys. "Now!"

As Linda and Alison run for cover, Ferdy emerges from his position as well.

As Protector 3 unleashes a volley of green laser blasts, Rick and Ferdy pull a blue sheet off of a large mirror positioned behind them. Just as everyone hoped, one of Protector 3's laser beams bounces back at it, cracking its visor and frying its CPU. The robot hisses and sizzles as webs of electricity arc over its entire body.

"ERROR!" reports Protector 3.

It fires erratically as it spins, all four arms flailing. It may be incapacitated, but it's still deadly.

As Ferdy and Alison take cover against a wall, Rick runs out of the department store, determined to knock Protector 3's lights out permanently. He fires mercilessly.

"Go to Robot Hell!" he hollers.

"Rick!" Linda yells. "Be careful."

The semi-blind Protector zeros in on Linda's voice and blasts her square in the torso. She screams as she falls backwards, a green inferno cooking her body from the inside out. She's a dead husk before she even hits the ground.

"Linda!" Rick screams like a wounded animal. He turns back towards the malfunctioning Protector. "You son of a bitch!" He sees an orange service cart parked close by and hops in. He turns the electric vehicle on, points it at Protector 3, and floors the accelerator. "I'll kill you!" he screams like a mad conqueror.

"Rick!" Alison screams. "No!"

Rick doesn't listen. He's determined to pulverize the robot who killed his wife—even if it's a kamikaze mission. He smashes into Protector 3 with enough force to crumple the robot and the cart.

Unfortunately, the moment the metal cart makes contact with the arcing robot, webs of electricity engulf them both.

Rick screams as his body seizes. Thousands of watts surge through his body, searing veins and arteries and causing his internal organs to burst. His entire body begins to glow.

"Rick!" Ferdy yells. He and Alison both shrink in horror.

There's a loud *pop* followed by a cloud of ozone. The electrical surge ceases and Rick tumbles out of the cart, dead. Boiling blood gushes from his mouth.

Protector 3 explodes in a blinding flash, a burst of smoke, and a million sparks.

Rick's lifeless body continues to smolder and pop.

It is more than Ferdy can stand.

"Rick!" he moans, falling to his knees. "No!"

Alison crouches down beside him.

"Let's go find that computer and kill these motherfuckers," Ferdy says.

CHAPTER 30

Ferdy and Alison scan the third level of Park Plaza, hoping to spot the master control room.

"Where the hell is it?" Alison asks.

"I don't know," Ferdy replies. "It's probably hidden in one of these service corridors."

"There's hundreds of doors back there," Alison says. "We'll never find it!"

"We have to!" Ferdy replies. "We're sitting ducks otherwise."

"Okay, well, you try the north side, and I'll try the south side."

"I don't want to split up!" Ferdy says.

"We have to. Otherwise, we're wasting time," Alison says. "I don't want one of us to die because we couldn't shut the computer down in time. We've gotta try!"

"All right. But if you see anything or hear anything-"

"Believe me," Alison interrupts. "You'll hear me."

"Okay," Ferdy replies.

They hug.

"Be careful," Ferdy says.

"You too."

They reach an entrance to the service corridors and head off in opposite directions.

Alison stumbles into a wing that looks like it's still under construction.

Since the control room is new, maybe its somewhere in this area, she thinks, navigating through vines of hanging wires and building debris.

Alison finds herself in a storage area. She jumps when she hears a muffled clank coming from behind a doorway. Is it someone in the control room, a potential ally—or a rabid robot lying in wait?

Only one way to find out, Alison thinks.

She finds a three-foot piece of copper piping leaning up against the wall. She grabs it, clutches one end, and holds it up like a baseball bat. Carefully, vigilantly, Alison moves towards the door. Her hand trembles as she reaches for the knob.

As soon as she cracks the door, a small avalanche of construction debris tumbles out, creating quite a racket. There's no control room, no potential ally, and (most importantly) no killer robots. She's relieved and even laughs at herself—but no one's out of the woods yet. Not even close.

Alison finds herself in another storeroom, this one filled with shelves of electronics supplies. There's an open door on the other side of the room. *Is that the control room?* she wonders. She's so focused, she doesn't hear Protector 1 silently stalking her from behind.

"DETAIN INTRUDER!" the robot raises all four of its arms and snaps its claws menacingly.

Alison turns and screams.

"Ferdy!" The robot has her cornered; she slowly backs up against a wall. "Ferdy! Ferdy! Help!"

The robot is almost in striking distance. Protector 1 extends a snapping claw towards Alison's throat.

"Ferdy!" she screams at the top of her lungs.

Ferdy bursts into the storeroom like a superhero.

"Alison, move!" he shouts, pointing his gun at the robot. "Get out!"

Alison jumps out of the way as Ferdy pops shots at Protector 1. Most bullets simply turn to dust when they hit the robot's chrome and titanium shell, but Ferdy gets lucky. He manages to strike Protector 1's visor, shattering it and severely limiting its functionality.

"Laser malfunction," Protector 1 says. "Laser malfunction. Detain intruder. Detain intruder!"

Ferdy and Alison dash through the service corridors and back onto the third level of the mall.

Protector 1 may not be able to see clearly, and its lasers are permanently offline, but it should still be able to finish off its last two targets.

"Laser malfunction!" it repeats as it hauls after Ferdy and Alison. "Laser malfunction! Detain intruders! Detain anti-consumers!"

"What should we do now?" Alison asks, out of breath. "Keep looking for the control room?"

"I don't know," Ferdy says.

There's no time to think.

Protector 1 comes bursting out of the service corridor. "Detain intruders!"

"He can only follow one of us," Alison tells Ferdy.

Ferdy nods as they break off in opposite directions again.

"Detain intruders." Protector follows after Ferdy, who is almost instantly cornered.

With nowhere to run, Ferdy backs up against a railing and looks over the ledge. There's no way he'd survive if he jumps.

"DETAIN INTRUDERS!"

Protector 1 continues closing in.

Ferdy shoots his last few bullets at the robot. When the gun is empty, he tosses it like a hand grenade. It bounces ineffectually off Protector 1's shell.

"STOP RIGHT THERE," Protector 1 says.

"Ferdy!" Alison appears, seemingly from out of nowhere.

"Alison!" he yells. "Get the hell out of here!" That's when he notices a fire-extinguisher mounted on a wall. It's within arm's reach. He grabs the red canister and hurls it at the robot with all his might.

The fire extinguisher lands uselessly at the base of Protector 1's wheels.

It was *not* a good shot.

In a single fluid motion, Protector 1 picks up the fire extinguisher and hurls it back at Ferdy with incredible power.

The fire extinguisher connects with Ferdy's skull. His feet fall out from under him and he hits the tile, completely motionless.

Alison sees blood gushing from Ferdy's head.

"No!" she screams.

Protector 1 stands over Ferdy, surveying the damage.

"THANK YOU. HAVE A NICE DAY."

CHAPTER 31

Protector 1 turns its attention to Alison—its final target.

Alison turns and sprints away as fast as she can; so fast, she gets a stitch in her side. She turns a corner, momentarily out of Protector 1's range. Before it can catch up to her, Alison picks up an ashtray and smashes the front window of Roger's Little Shop of Pets.

It's a fitting place for a game of cat and mouse.

Protector 1 still can't see clearly, but its sensors are alerted to the sound of breaking glass. The robot calculates the location of the disturbance and sets course towards Roger's Little Shop of Pets.

Alison knows the robot will find her soon if she doesn't hide. She races past rows of fishtanks and terrariums towards the back of the store. Dozens of dogs in glass kennels begin barking and howling.

Protector 1 turns a corner and notes the freshly broken glass outside of Rogers.

Inside, Alison stuffs herself into the bottom shelf of a dog food display. She hears the robot rolling into the store; she hears its neck turning as it surveys the environment, looking for anything out of place.

As it moves from the front of the store to the back, Protector 1 knocks over a terrarium full of giant tarantulas, then another terrarium filled with boa constrictors. The critters scamper and slither across the floor in all directions—including towards Alison's hiding place.

Soon, half a dozen tarantulas are crawling across Alison's sweater and into her hair. Snakes slide across her ankles and in between her legs. It's all she can do to keep from screaming out in horror. She pulls a bag of dog food over her face and prays.

Protector 1 finally leaves the store.

Alison emerges slowly and carefully from her hiding place. She kicks away the snakes and shakes the spiders off her sweater and out of her hair. She's completely grossed out, but knows she's got worse things to worry about than innocent animals—even the scary looking ones.

She's about to slip out of Roger's when a black cat named Mandy jumps from her perch on a shelf and into Alison's arms. Startled, Alison lets a scream slip—just a little one. Still, it was enough to stop Protector 1 in its tracks.

"DETAIN INTRUDER," it says before doubling back towards the pet store. It sees Alison slipping out and picks up speed. "DETAIN INTRUDER!" It snaps its claws relentlessly. "DETAIN INTRUDER!"

Alison sprints around a corner.

When Protector 1 turns the same corner—she's gone. It rolls slowly down the causeway.

"ACTIVATING MOTION DETECTION," Protector 1 says.

Alison is hiding, but she's far from safe. She's hanging over the side of the walkway on the railing's lowest rung. She knows that if she slips, the three-story fall will kill her—and her hands are getting sweaty.

She pulls her head up over the lip of the ledge in order to track the robot's movements. When it moves one way, she moves the other. Every time she releases one of her hands, however, it becomes harder to keep her grip.

Protector 1 catches a glimpse of Alison's hands and moves in to investigate.

"DETAIN INTRUDER!"

This is it. Alison realizes she's probably dead no matter what she does.

Alison lets go of the railing. Time seems to slow as she races towards the ground at one-hundred miles per hour. She thinks about Ferdy right before impact.

Amazingly, improbably, Alison's fall is broken by the canvas canopy of a kiosk of knickknacks and geeky apparel called Corman's Curiosities. The tent-like structure slows her fall before crumpling in on itself. Boxes of toys and other items scatter about the floor around her.

Alison is alive and nothing is broken, but she's still hurt. She's never had the wind knocked out of her quite like this before. She's struggling just to breathe, still too shaken to even stand up.

From the third level, Protector 1 looks down at her.

"DETAIN INTRUDER."

"Fuck yourself," she screams back weakly.

"DETAIN INTRUDER."

Alison watches as Protector 1 catches an escalator; it's one of the long ones that goes all the way from Level Three to Level One without stoping at Level Two.

"Oh, God," Alison moans. She knows the robot will catch up to her in a matter of moments. *It's time to get rid of this fucker once and for all!*

She crawls along the tile floor of the first level until she's out of the robot's direct line of sight.

She quickly reaches a dead end, finding herself up against the locked doors of a paint store, The Paint and the Pendulum. She has nowhere else to run (or crawl). She's hopelessly trapped.

Alison turns over on her back and stares up at the ceiling, utterly defeated.

She can hear Protector 1 getting closer.

"Detain Intruder."

Alison wonders if Protector 1 will kill her quickly, like Leslie and Greg, or slowly like Suzie. She hopes it'll be merciful on her. She clutches her hands against her chest and notices something she's forgotten about.

"Send up a flare and I'll come running," Alison says.

She still has the flare she took from the hardware store. It gives her an idea.

Alison crawls towards the front of The Paint and the Pendulum and pulls herself to her feet. She looks for something to break the window with. Seeing nothing close by, she pulls her sweater over her face and breaks the front window with her head.

Badass.

Protector 1 reaches the first level of Park Plaza. It hears the glass breaking and triangulates the location of the disturbance. It plots a course towards The Paint and the Pendulum.

"Detain intruder!"

Alison limps into the house paint section and begins pulling cans off the shelf. She finds a screwdriver and begins popping lids. She throws gallons of paint on the floor, one can after another. Sky blue, salmon pink, lemon yellow, lime green, lavender and more. It's a massive puddle of psychedelic swirls.

Next, Alison finds a row of highly flammable paint thinner. She grabs a can, unscrews the cap, and spills the contents onto the sizable paint puddle. Then she unscrews another can and does the same thing. Then she opens another can...

The toxic fumes are intense, almost stifling. Alison knows if she doesn't get out soon, she'll probably pass out.

Protector 1 is almost upon her.

"DETAIN INTRUDER."

"Come on, you little bastard!" Alison yells, taunting. "Come and get me!" She grabs her flare and hides in a corner of the store as Protector 1 rolls inside, crashing through the rest of the store's glass windows.

"DETAIN INTRUDER!"

"I'm right here!" Alison screams.

Protector 1 rolls towards her voice and right into the puddle of paint and industrial solvents. Its treads become slippery and it loses all traction. It spins in circles trying to correct course—just as Alison hoped it would.

She makes a break for it, scrambling to the front of the store and out the doors, nearly slipping in wet paint.

Alison turns around, sees Protector 1 still spinning. She lights her flare and looks at the flailing robot.

"Hey!"

Protector 1 turns its visor towards Alison.

"DETAIN INTRUDER."

"I don't think so," Alison replies before tossing the lit flair into the paint store. "*Have a nice day!*"

Alison's flare ignites a fireball that consumes Protector 1 in an instant. The explosion melts cans of paint and solvents, leading to additional, bigger explosions. The entire front of

The Paint and the Pendulum shatters, expelling toxic smoke, broken glass, and scraps of metal.

It's enough to throw Alison completely off her feet. She falls on her stomach and protects her head and neck with her hands, just like she'd been taught in earthquake drills at school. She feels the flames roaring overhead, singeing the fine hairs of her cashmere sweater.

Everything settles and grows quiet. Only the fire burning inside The Paint and the Pendulum remains.

Alison lifts her head and looks around. She finds one of Protector 1's charred claws nearby. She looks back into the store at what's left of the robot.

Its head has been severed from its neck, connected only by a few cables. Its arms are mangled, its lights have been blown out, and its shell is melting in the relentless blaze. Alison thinks it's one of the most beautiful things she's ever seen. She gets to her feet, smiling victoriously.

Alison limps her way towards the Plaza's main courtyard. The new morning sun shines through the mall's extensive system of skylights.

Someone calls out to her.

"Hey!"

It's Ferdy! He's alive! He's coming down a stairwell right towards her—holding a roll of toilet paper against the back of his head to soak up the blood.

"Ferdy!" Alison beams up at him.

"Nice shot!"

They run to one another.

The couple embraces as the mall's impenetrable security doors slide open.

EPILOGUE

Jamal Jerome slowly pulls himself out from the plaster rubble he's been passed out under for the last few hours. He's covered in white dust and there's a gash above his left eyebrow, but he's otherwise unhurt. He surveys what's left of his secret lair.

"Well," he sighs. "I guess I'm homeless again."

"May I see your ID badge, please," says an ominous voice from behind him.

Jamal spins around, coming face-to-visor with Protector 4.

"You gotta be fucking kidding!"

High above Park Plaza, locked in geosynchronous orbit, a sleek alien spacecraft hums against the void. Inside, two extraterrestrial observers watch the mall carnage unfold on an array of glowing monitors. Their experiment is complete.

With a flick of a clawed hand, they terminate the GOG protocol. The rogue AI that turned the *security* bots into relentless *kill* bots is no more. The aliens begin preparations for the long journey home, their work here done.

For decades, they've visited Earth, studying its inhabitants and meddling whenever the mood struck. Their latest trial—hijacking humanity's own technology against them—has exceeded their expectations.

Did they hope to teach us a lesson about the perils of artificial intelligence and tampering with forces we can't control? Or were their motives something else entirely?

One alien swivels a bulbous eye towards the other.

"Humans," it chortles, a gurgling laugh echoing through the cabin. "They're so much fun to fuck with."

The ship vanishes into the black, leaving Earth none the wiser.

The following pages feature images from the film *Chopping Mall*. Used by permission.

CHOPPING MALL
Where Shopping Costs You an Arm and a Leg!
STARRING
KELLI MARONEY
TONY O'DELL · JOHN TERLESKY
RUSSEL TODD · PAUL BARTEL
MARY WORONOV and DICK MILLER
WRITTEN BY
JIM WYNORSKI & STEVE MITCHELL
ROBOTS CREATED BY
ROBERT SHORT
PRODUCED BY
JULIE CORMAN
DIRECTED BY
JIM WYNORSKI
Park Plaza Mall
© 1986 CONCORDE/TRINITY PICTURES

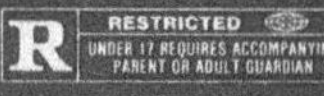

R RESTRICTED
UNDER 17 REQUIRES ACCOMPANYING
PARENT OR ADULT GUARDIAN

BUY OR DIE...
CHOPPING MALL
M
FOR MATURE AUDIENCES
Where shopping costs you
an arm and a leg!
Starring RUSSEL TODD (FRIDAY THE 13TH), BARBARA CRAMPTON (RE-ANIMATOR),
KELLI MARONEY (NIGHT OF THE COMET) and TONY O'DELL (THE KARATE KID).

CHOPPING
MALL

SLAVICK'S

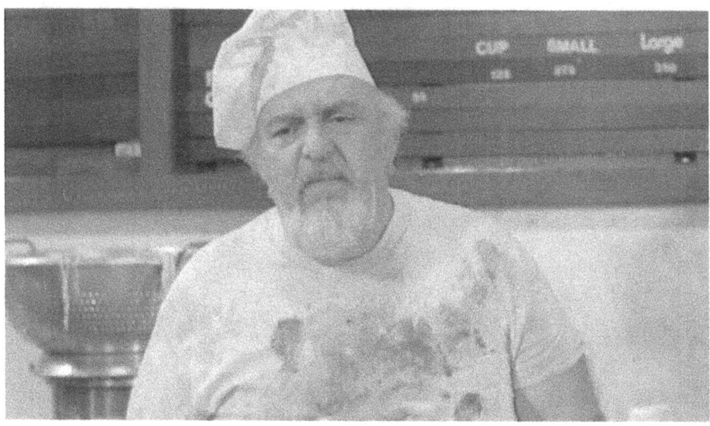
CUP   SMALL   Large

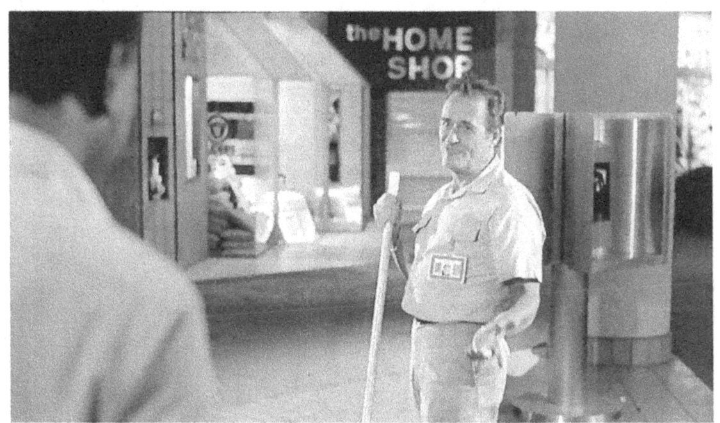
the HOME
SHOP

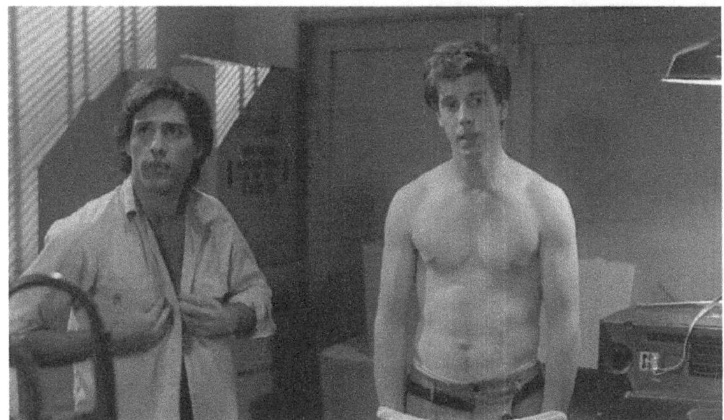

Wet Floor

Marita

ABOUT THE AUTHOR

Photo credit: *Ama Lea*

Over the past decade-plus, Joshua Millican has proven himself to be a horror expert of the highest caliber. After establishing a personal blog in 2011, Millican quickly became one of the horror genre's premiere journalists, contributing to many websites before ultimately landing at Dread Central in 2016. One of the top horror outlets on the planet, Millican served as Editor-in-Chief from 2019 through 2021. In addition to writing, Millican has been a member of numerous festival juries, a popular podcast guest, and has even scored a handful of acting gigs. His talk show *Chronic Horror* (sidelined by the Pandemic) explored the intersection of horror movie fandom and cannabis culture. Now married and a father for the first time, Millican pens hardcore horror/sci-fi/fantasy fiction like *Deeper Than Hell* and novelizations like *Forbidden Zone, Circus of the Dead, and All Through the House.*

ALSO BY JOSHUA MILLICAN

Deeper Than Hell

Septum: A Deeper Than Hell Paraquel

The Dreadful Years

Forbidden Zone: The Novelization

Teleportasm (published by Shortwave Publishing)

All Through the House: The Novelization

Circus of the Dead: The Novelization

9 781966 037064